the
second
first
time

the second first time

A NOVEL

ELISA LORELLO

LAKE UNION
PUBLISHING

Text copyright © 2016 Elisa Lorello
All rights reserved.

Excerpt from and paraphrases of the following article appear in the text: Mandy Len Catron, "To Fall in Love with Anyone, Do This," *New York Times*, January 9, 2015. Updated February 13, 2015, http://www.nytimes.com/2015/01/11/fashion/modern-love-to-fall-in-love-with-anyone-do-this.html?_r=0

The *New York Times* article was based on the following study: Arthur Aron et. al, "The Experimental Generation of Interpersonal Closeness: A Procedure and Some Preliminary Findings," *Personality and Social Psychology Bulletin* 23, no. 4 (1997): 363–377. © 1997 by the Society for Personality and Social Psychology.

Published by Lake Union Publishing, Seattle

www.apub.com

ISBN-13: 9781503941243
ISBN-10: 1503941248

Cover design by Michael Rehder

Printed in the United States of America

For Craig
May this glorious road trip never end.

Chapter One

The day after Thanksgiving

If you saw a chick in blue jeans and T-shirt with a cardigan and Chucks and an oversize pleather purse, having a fabulous hair day, and sporting a goofy grin in Sag Harbor on Black Friday, that was me.

Sixty-five degrees in November on the East End. *Sixty-five degrees!* The day after Thanksgiving! And sunny. The town was bustling with Manhattan residents visiting and celebrities staying in their Hamptons homes for the holiday weekend and getting a jump start on Christmas shopping in the boutiques that lined the mile-long Main Street. My mother lives here year-round, in a modest bungalow by Hamptons standards (the property taxes are surprisingly low), and tells my sister Gaia and me that when she dies we can either sell it, rent it in the summer—we could easily get twenty grand for July and August—or use it as a summer home for ourselves. Port Jefferson, where I currently live, has many of the same attributes as "the Sag," but it's more crowded on just about any given day, and parking in the village is a slice of hell.

My point is that today was one of those perfect days when everything is right in your world and everything in your entire life brought you to this moment of simplicity. When you sing the closing song to *Mister Rogers' Neighborhood* and feel every word vibrating in your aura. Maybe it was the weather. Maybe it was the sugar high from the leftover pecan pie for breakfast. Maybe it was the e-mail from my editor sending me the contract for my latest novel, *Change at Jamaica.* Maybe because Thanksgiving just makes you grateful.

Or maybe it was just life, finally balancing itself out, telling me, "You're OK, kid."

It took me almost the entire year to get to this place. Finishing the novel was a huge help. Gave me a channel for the heartbreak, the disappointment, even the anger. A chance to get back into the fantasy dating pool, which is way more fun than the real one. I even managed to find the funny. My friends and fellow authors, Hazel Scott and Kalvin T. Roberts ("the *T* is for Thomas"), also helped.

"You know, you can do really mean things to a person in fiction," Kalvin had said following the relationship implosion. "Why do you think I'm so well adjusted?"

Believe me, I knew. And I did.

The rest was just day by day—the melting of snow, the coming of spring, the return of the sun. Not to mention Sag Harbor in all its splendor. God, I want to live here.

Heck, maybe I was even ready to start dating again. For real.

My purse buzzed. I stopped in my tracks to locate the muffled ring and fish out my phone before it stopped, but I was too late. When I finally found it and looked at the screen, the phone buzzed in my hand, alerting me to a text message from Gaia: Call me. Urgent.

Was it coincidence that a cloud covered the sun at that moment, or foreshadowing? Regardless, my mood dimmed as well.

I dialed and she picked up on the first ring.

"Sorry to bother you," she said. Traditionally we came into town together on Black Friday, but she had a cold. And yet I could tell the strain in her voice had nothing to do with any physical malady.

"What's wrong?" I asked.

"Kathleen just called. Dad died."

Chapter Two

There's always a defining moment in your life where, if you had to do it over, you'd go back and change the trajectory. As a writer, I can spend hours on the hypotheticals of how I'd redo the moment my father left when I was ten years old and Gaia was twelve. Left us for Kathleen. Not Kathy. Not Kate. *Kathleen.* What I'd say, how I'd respond, whether I would have become a hairstylist anyway or instead completed an MFA in some prestigious writing program and become a published novelist before the age of forty. But of course, it's all predicated on what I know now, not what I knew then. And really, what kind of power does a ten-year-old have over something like that?

We hadn't seen our father since he moved out west about twenty years ago. Phone calls on birthdays and holidays soon devolved to e-mails, and two years ago, not even that.

"When?" I asked Gaia.

"Monday. Stroke. It was instant."

"*Monday?* And she's just getting around to calling us now?"

"Said she didn't want to ruin our holiday."

First thought: *Thanksgivings are gonna suck from now on.* Odd how you always start with the superficial before the impact sinks in.

I'd thought something equally superficial when the twin towers came down: *The skyline will look terrible now.*

"What about funeral plans?"

"None," said Gaia. "Can you believe it? Kathleen went and cremated him without bothering to tell his children that he died. She probably went out to dinner immediately afterward."

My jaw dropped for a solid five seconds. I was beyond shocked. Dumbfounded. Flabbergasted.

"Are you shitting me?" I asked a little louder than I'd intended, drawing looks from nearby pedestrians exiting the Golden Pear café.

"I'm not sure I would have gone anyway," said Gaia. "But so much for getting closure."

Sadly, I'd wondered from time to time about what I'd do when our father passed away—whether I'd travel across the country out of obligation or pay my respects by making a donation to a charity in his name. Gaia and I had wondered if going to his funeral would give us some kind of closure, as she said, or if *closure* was a leftover buzzword from counseling in the eighties.

Regardless, the decision was made for me. I would have preferred to live with indecision—or the wrong decision—rather than once again have my life usurped by Kathleen, who was the human equivalent of a black hole.

"Me neither," I said, and did a panorama of the town—autumn leaves clinging to branches and scattered around tree trunks; women dressed in perky baby-doll tops and skinny jeans holding hands with men in nautical polo shirts and carpenter shorts, sunglasses shading their eyes while showcasing their smiles. Gay and straight couples alike walking little dogs. Blue skies providing color contrast to brick buildings. Diagonal rows of parked convertibles. Everyone looked the way I felt just seconds before I picked up my phone.

Suddenly I didn't want to be alone.

"Gaia, I'm going to come over now. OK with you?"

"Of course."

We said our good-byes and I tapped the screen, slipped the phone into my purse, and headed for my Beetle parked on the other side of Main Street. From there I drove to Gaia's house in Riverhead. She and I had banded together on those first nights following our father's departure, when Mom was so distraught she burned dinner, leaving us to make buttered toast or PB&J. We'd shared a room, and I used to crawl into her bed, where we'd cry into a pillow so Mom didn't hear us.

Or maybe I just wanted to be surrounded by a solid family unit. Kevin felt like a best buddy more than a brother-in-law, and Erika was my playmate as much as she was my niece.

Today, Gaia and I didn't cry. Didn't even hug. Just sat on the couch in the den and speculated on what Dad's life had been like these last few years, since we lost all contact with him.

"Maybe they finally got out and traveled," I said. "Can you imagine Dad and Kathleen at Disney World decked out in Hawaiian shirts and mouse ears?"

"Maybe Kathleen needlepointed him to death," said Gaia.

"What do you think things would have been like had he and Mom stayed together?" We asked each other this question about once every five years.

Gaia gave her usual answer. "I don't know. Either Mom would have been less active or Dad would have been more active. No way would she have put up with his nitpickiness."

"There's a reason why Dad and Kathleen ended up together," I said. "She was a perfect reflection of him."

Maybe it was because I'd been so young when Dad left, but I hadn't remembered him as nitpicky. He was always aloof—with words, affection, praise—but he was, if nothing else, polite. And musical. He was a different person when playing an instrument, and he could play just about any instrument he picked up. In hindsight, it was the only time I ever saw him smile.

"Want to stay and get a pizza or something?" Gaia asked.

"Sure," I said. She called Kevin, who was spending the day with Erika, and asked him to pick up a pie on their way home.

You wouldn't have guessed that we'd just learned about our father's death, the way we all laughed and carried on as we normally did. First stage of grief was denial, right? Maybe that's what we were doing. Or maybe there wasn't much else to do. We had grieved the loss of our father years ago.

After playing three games of Acey-Deucey with Erika (she kicked my butt) and finishing off the last of the chocolate chip cookies she had baked yesterday, I gathered my sweater, purse, and keys.

"Going home?" asked Gaia.

"Where else is there to go?"

"You could stay here."

"And catch your icky cold? No, thanks."

She huffed. "Too late for that." She paused for a beat. "What about Mom?"

"What about her?"

"We should tell her. She has a right to know. And maybe she'll need some comfort."

"You think I should spend the night there?"

Big sister that she was, Gaia practically ordered me to do so.

I called Mom and told her I was heading back to her house. Then I thanked Gaia and Kevin for the pizza and hugged them and Erika. From there I drove back to Sag Harbor as my brain rapidly spun a cycle of thoughts, memories, and images. My dad walking out the door—no fight, no announcement (at least not to Gaia or me)—suitcase in hand, kissing us good-bye as if he were leaving for a business trip and not the rest of our lives. Mom locked in her bedroom, so eerily quiet, as if she were invisible. And maybe she'd felt that way. The walls caving in as he departed, leaving us in the rubble. I don't think it would have been so crushing had it not been such a shock. There hadn't been a trace of discontent in my parents' marriage, at least none that my ten-year-old senses could detect, and kids tend to be pretty perceptive about such things, despite parents thinking they're doing a good job shielding their kids from it.

Mom was waiting at the door when I trudged up the walkway. "What couldn't you tell me over the phone?"

I entered the house and spied a plate of zeppoli sitting on the kitchen island.

"Kathleen called Gaia late this morning. Dad's dead," I said. Might as well tell it like it was.

Mom turned her head away, staring into nothingness, and in that one second I saw her mentally relive her courtship and marriage and divorce and postdivorce. A woman in her early twenties, fresh out of college, with a beehive hairdo and painted eyeliner and a polka-dotted dress with clunky pumps. A man with olive-toned skin, tall and lean, who looked a little like Frank Sinatra in the early years. Debonair. Her, a bookkeeper-turned-homemaker-turned-counselor. Him, a microwave-engineer-turned-solar-engineer-turned-defense-contractor-turned-adulterer. Two little girls raised on Barbie and *Charlie's Angels* and Dr. Scholl's sandals and disco in the seventies giving way to Love's Baby Soft and *Miami Vice* and British new wave come the eighties.

I don't think Gaia and I knew that Dad cheated on Mom with Kathleen until we were in our midteens, when Mom told us. But we *knew*. We always knew. Not that he left clues or said anything explicit. But I remembered a seashell he'd brought home one day. He wasn't a seashell-collecting guy. He took it out, looked at it, and threw it in the trash. He never knew I was watching him. I'd thought it was pretty, so I fished it out, washed it, and put it back on the table. An hour later, it was back in the trash, smashed. To this day I don't know who smashed it, him or Mom.

Mom and I both returned from our reveries. "I'm sorry to hear it," she said.

"She told us *after* he was cremated. How's that for consideration?"

Mom rolled her eyes. "Predictable." She ran her hand along my hair and pushed it behind my ear. "You OK, sweetie bear?"

I shrugged my shoulders. "I guess so. Are *you* OK?"

"It was another lifetime ago," she said. "Whoever passed away this week wasn't the man I married. I wish him peace, though."

"Whatever," I replied. "Gaia the mother hen didn't want me to be alone tonight, but now that I'm here, I kind of want my own bed. No offense."

She hugged me. "None taken."

With her formerly brunette beehive now a sassy silver-white pixie (a style I recommended and administered), perfect for the shape of her face, she adjusted her glasses and peered at me. "You sure you're OK?"

"Peachy," I said, and made a direct line to the zeppoli. One for the road.

I didn't flip on the lights when I got home. Just trudged through the house to my bedroom, where I flopped onto the bed, propped the navy-blue pillows against the headboard, and leaned back in the darkness, staring beyond the opaque window.

My father: gone. Again. There was a new finality that hadn't existed before.

I needed to tell someone. But what did I want to say? What story did I want to tell?

I flicked on the light and hopped off the bed, bare feet slapping against the cold hardwood floor as I padded to the closet. The keepsake box on the top shelf had accumulated some dust, evidence that I hadn't opened it in a while. I wiped the top with my sleeve, lifted the lid, and extracted its contents: a yo-yo that I'd won in second grade for the best drawing of my favorite zoo animal (a panda bear); programs from all my piano recitals from junior high through high school; my first pair of haircutting scissors (they'd cost twenty bucks at the drugstore); and the thing I'd been looking for—a faded, frayed photo of my dad and me on Christmas Day, 1976, next to a new Schwinn, the Mercedes of bicycles. Whereas my smile revealed the gap in my front teeth, his seemed to be hiding something. I never could tell if he was happy.

I manipulated the photo left and right, looking at it from different angles. Looking at *him*. Looking for any clue that he'd been planning to leave all along. Wondering if, had I been able to detect that clue, I could have somehow prevented him from leaving.

And then I spied the letter, at the bottom of the box, underneath the concert ticket stubs and my mortarboard tassel. I'd buried it back in March.

It was possible I'd been looking for that too.

I unearthed it and ran my fingers across the stock envelope before removing the paper from inside and unfolding it. The return address: Tacoma, Washington. The corners were starting to crinkle.

Jonathan's handwriting was so familiar now, scripted penmanship you don't see anymore. Come to think of it, you don't see handwritten letters on stationery either.

> *Dearest Sage,*
> *I'm awake at 4:18 a.m. to write to you because I realized, in my sleeplessness, that there are things I know and don't know.*
>
> *What I know: My thoughts orient to you, every day, at all hours, at random, and in those moments—fleeting these days—when I have myself together. When I'm in trouble, you're the first person I think of to help me through it. When I have good news to share, you're the one with whom I wish to share it. When I lay my head down at night, I*

send up a thought to you, that your head is resting peacefully. When I wake up, I want to talk to you. You're the only person I've ever wanted to see all of me.

"I love you." I've always had to be told those words repeatedly to appease my insecurity rather than as an affirmation of intimacy. All my life I've lived with the fucked-up fear that no one would really love me, the terror that even if I found it, I would somehow lose it. But in a moment of genuine friendship, you said those very words and I believed it, with every particle of my being, and I realized that I'll never have to question it with you.

I know we have an opportunity with this road trip that few people get: the chance to start our journey together from a place of absolute and enduring honesty. That the dumb shit we've done in our pasts doesn't have to be part of what we build together.

What I don't know: how long my heart will remain lacerated. I don't know when my confidence and existential joy will return. I don't know how this all works. The distance scares me. The merging of two independent, strong-willed lives is daunting, and not knowing exactly how to do it makes me feel vulnerable. And that is precisely why I can't take this trip with you. Not now. Not yet.

I know it may seem as if I am abandoning you, and I am deeply sorry if you are feeling pain as you read this letter. But please know this, because I know it: You are my friend, Sage Merriweather. My best friend. You always will be. And I always want to be yours. But as your best friend, I couldn't live with myself if I jumped into something with you that I wasn't ready for. Something that, *in the right time and place and circumstance, would be nothing short of magical. Graceful. Delicious. I'm not running away from you. I'm running toward myself. And I hope you'll be there when I arrive.*

    Yours, Jon

I'd been flummoxed when I first read the letter, soon to be one year ago to the day. Felt the same walls cave in on me as when my father left.

And yet it was the most beautiful letter anyone had ever written me.

Sure, he lived on the other side of the country, and we'd only been in a room together once. Over two years ago. At a publisher's party in Manhattan. Surrounded by drunk authors. But following that party we'd become the modern-day Julia Child and Avis DeVoto, beginning first with comment threads on Facebook posts before switching to long e-mails and two-hour conversations either via Messenger or text or FaceTime. We sent photos of what we ate for lunch that day and read excerpts from the day's word count of whatever manuscripts we were slaving over. We even jammed long-distance—he on guitar, me on piano.

Best buddies.

And then he got divorced. And, oddly enough, that signaled the beginning of the end for us too.

How long had it been since we'd last spoken in person? Would he speak to me now? Why, after all this time, did I want to call Jonathan Moss?

Because *when I'm in trouble, you're the first person I think of to help me through it.* Still.

I grabbed my phone, searched the contacts list, and found his name. I'd never deleted him.

I touched the screen and waited, mentally composing what I might say if the call went to voice mail.

My stomach somersaulted with every ring. Until I heard his voice. Then it vaulted into my throat.

"Hi, Sage."

"Hi, Jon."

Was he shocked? Angry? Indifferent? I couldn't tell.

"How are you?" he asked.

"My father died."

And then the deluge of tears finally came.

CHAPTER THREE

Jonathan waited patiently while I bawled until I finally stopped and sobbed, "I'm sorry."

"It's OK," he said. He offered his condolences and I thanked him. "When did he pass?"

"Monday," I replied. "He had a stroke. His wife called my sister this morning. *After* she had him cremated."

"Damn," he said. "That's awful."

"She's a dybbuk, Jon. If I wrote a character based on her, I'd be criticized for being too unrealistic and over-the-top."

"I'm sorry," he said. "Truly. Had anything changed between you and your dad these last few months?"

I shook my head as if he were sitting opposite me. "No. I can't remember the last time I spoke to him. The last time I even cared. And now . . . now I can't do anything about that. But you know what really upsets me? It's that I didn't *want* to."

"Can you really blame yourself for that? He had just as many opportunities to do something about it."

"I could have been the bigger person. But I just . . . I don't know. Every time I considered it, I turned ten again."

How could it be that, even though Jonathan and I hadn't spoken to each other for the better part of one year, I could talk to him so easily now? How could I feel so much like myself with someone who had done the one thing I had never forgiven my father for—leaving me?

"It's going to be OK, Sage," he said. "It totally sucks right now, but you're going to get through it."

I wiped my eyes, followed by my nose, relieved we weren't on FaceTime. "You must think I'm nuts to call you out of the blue like this," I said.

"Not at all. Surprised, yes. Even glad, although I would have preferred it to be because of happier circumstances." He paused for a beat. "May I ask why you called *me*?"

The letter was still in my hand. "Because . . ." I started, and took a deep breath. "Because I want to make something right."

I wasn't sure what the "wrong" was—trying to forge a romance where none was to be found, thus ruining our friendship, or killing a romance before it even got off the ground. Or both.

A pregnant pause took over, and just as I was sure the call had been bounced, he said, "I've missed you. I've missed our friendship."

My heart pounded. I'd longed to hear those words, dreamed about them many times. His admission was a key to a door I'd locked, and even though I was afraid to open it again, I couldn't help but turn that key. "Me too," I confessed. "Do you think maybe we could . . . *talk* to each other again?"

"You mean outside of social media comments?"

Last week, in response to our mutual friend and fellow author Hazel Scott's post about demanding that one of the Macy's Thanksgiving Day Parade balloons be a TARDIS, Jonathan and I had gone off on a tangent of "Rejected Balloons," including a beverage-out-his-nose-inducing comment by yours truly—"giant middle finger"—followed by his "Curious George Bush." I had initiated the thread, but Jon had jumped right in, and next thing we knew, we'd forgotten about Hazel as the primary audience. It was the first time we'd interacted with each other in any capacity since the phone call following the letter last year. The exchange had been reminiscent of the formerly frequent banter we'd become so accustomed to and comfortable with—making up our own *Onion*-inspired article headlines ("Local Author Confesses His Only Friends Are Cats," "Long Island Girl Snubs Neighboring States' Bagels"); revising movie lines ("We're gonna need a bigger boat," formerly "We're going to need a larger flotation transport vehicle in order to catch the deadly sea creature"; "You can't handle the truth!" formerly "I'm not inclined to accommodate you!"); and replacing *Love* in song titles with *Shit* ("Addicted to Shit," "She Shits You," "Groovy Kind of Shit"). Jon was my midmorning-writing-coffee-break buddy, my watch-sports-from-our-respective-couches-and-text-while-doing-so companion, and, when I needed feedback, my most trusted beta reader. After he and his wife, Shannon, separated, we'd talk on the phone first thing in the morning and last thing at night. It had gotten to the point where I didn't need an alarm to wake up; the ringtone I'd used for Jonathan (the opening bars to Jimi Hendrix's "Purple Haze") took its place.

Whereas I was an eastern island girl, he was a western mountain boy. Whereas I was New Romantic, he was Classic Rock. Whereas I was a cat lover, he was a dog lover.

But we were both storytellers through and through. We shared an outlook on life, on *living*, that went beyond dialect or experience or politics or spirituality or moral values. We'd each charted the course of our lives, and we'd somehow met each other on the map.

And for a brief time, we'd traveled on the same road. Metaphorically speaking, that is.

Seconds after the exchange on Hazel's page, Jonathan had sent me a private message: That was fun. Like the good ol' days. Even though I'd desperately missed that banter and more, the fear of getting lured back into the friendship—or rather, onto the emotional roller coaster—superseded sentimentality, and I wound up copping out with a thumbs-up icon and no further communication.

Communication on social media was one thing. What I was asking for—to *talk*—was way bigger, and we both knew it. "Well, yes," I said. "Not FaceTime. But, you know, like we used to in the early days."

"I'd like that a lot," he said.

"Me too," I replied, despite an inner voice screaming, *Are you nuts? Why are you opening the door to this guy just so he can slam it on you again? The scar is still fresh. You're going to expose it?*

Yes. Yes, I was. Because I was nuts. Or stupid.

Or maybe I'd had enough of missing my friend. Death has a way of making you regret things. Or making you fix things before regret has a chance to sink in.

"So," I started, following another pause, "what's new with you?"

We both chortled. He was quick to amiably volley the ball back.

"No complaints. *Bleacher Seats* is up for a Best of the Year Award in the Contemporary Fiction category."

"Awesome," I said. "And well deserved. You know I loved that book. It's my favorite of yours."

I could almost hear him smiling. "Thanks."

My muscles tensed with every passing second of awkward silence. Throughout the course of our friendship, Jon and I had had either good communication or no communication. But never difficult. Until now.

He voiced my thoughts. "Maybe we need some practice."

"I'm sorry," I said.

"For what?"

"I don't know."

He paused again. "So, I was thinking . . ."

"About what?"

"Never mind. It's late. You must be exhausted."

I looked at the clock. And suddenly, in the way Wile E. Coyote doesn't know he's in midair until the Road Runner signals him to look down, my eyelids turned into anvils and a yawn broke out.

I apologized for the yawn, but he dismissed it. "Can I call you sometime tomorrow?" he asked.

"Sure," I said. "That would be nice."

"OK," he said. "Good night, Merriweather."

"Good night, Moss."

Oh, how I'd missed exchanging those words with him.

We ended the call and I turned out the light and pulled the covers snug around me.

Ten minutes later, my phone rang.

Jonathan.

"Did you forget something?" I said, forgoing *Hello*.

"So this may be the worst timing ever, but I got a crazy-ass idea," he said. "What do you say we take that road trip we were supposed to do last year?"

CHAPTER FOUR

You know when your heart somehow lodges itself in your throat and you feel like you're going to choke? Yeah, that's what happened the moment Jon proposed his idea.

The original road trip had been born as the result of us wanting to collaborate on a novel. We'd brainstormed a *Planes, Trains, and Automobiles* meets *French Kiss* romantic comedy of errors, enabling us to combine our specialties—mine being the rom-com side, and his being slice-of-life contemporary fiction. As research we'd decided to make the drive ourselves, scouting locations to use in the novel and having a blast along the way. It was also meant to be therapeutic for Jon, who had been reeling from divorce after finding out his wife of ten years had cheated on him.

Prior to his divorce, I'd never considered Jonathan Moss anything other than a friend. Had never found him sexually attractive. Had never contemplated a what-if. I'd met Shannon the same night Jon and I had met in New York City, and my first impression was that they seemed well suited. We never talked about his marriage or my love relationships in depth, however—a boundary I enforced with my married male friends. It was only after Jon and Shannon separated that he'd disclosed their having been in counseling, and even though he'd had suspicions, he was still devastated to learn about her affair. Once that boundary came down, however, the level of our closeness soared. Heck, I'd never even called him "Jon" until then.

The more we planned the road trip, the more it became a symbol of something else. Something we found ourselves wanting. The what-if: *What if we were more than friends? What if we'd been meant to be more than friends all along?* Writers are very good at imagining the what-if.

Had we been headed in that direction all along, or had the circumstances skewed the outcome?

"Seriously?" I said, turning on the light and sitting up in bed.

"I know—crazy, right? Believe it or not, it's something I've been thinking about since that exchange we had on Hazel's Facebook thread. Maybe even longer. But I've been too chickenshit to pitch it to you."

That he'd been thinking about it—about *us*—rattled me. Why hadn't he said anything sooner? Then again, if he had, I might have rejected it. Twenty-four hours ago I was living in a world where I thought I'd finally moved on from Jonathan Moss.

"I don't know," I said. "It's so out of the blue. For me, anyway."

"I understand. And maybe it's completely inappropriate timing."

Was there ever good timing for a guy who broke your heart to ask for a second helping?

"Just out of curiosity, when would it take place?" I asked.

"Exact same time as it was supposed to last year. Week of New Year's. Same start and end points: Phoenix and Tacoma. New Year's Eve in Sacramento, which kind of sucks, but San Francisco will be too expensive."

"My dad lives in Sacramento," I reminded him. "Lived."

Jon paused, no doubt to let the embarrassment seep in. "Fuck," he said.

"It's OK," I said. "I've never been there, so I'll take your word that it's a shitty place to spend New Year's Eve."

"I only meant in comparison to San Francisco." He paused again. "I'm digging a deeper hole here, huh."

"Not really," I said, but moved on. "When do we end up in Tacoma?"

"The day after New Year's. You can fly back to New York from Washington on the third or fourth, I guess. Up to you. Oh, and this would all be on my dime. Even your flights."

Holy shit. *His* dime? I couldn't tell if that made me more willing or more resistant.

"Wow," I said. "That's very generous of you."

"All you have to do is show up."

His words flashed back in my own voice, because they had once been *my* words, almost one year ago, when he began exhibiting signs of cold feet. *All you have to do is show up,* I'd said to him reassuringly. Oh, how easily we blind and deafen ourselves to the screaming signs—his repeated warnings that his heart was still shattered. His repeated mentions of Shannon. Erratic talk spanning from wanting to date other people to never wanting to date again.

"Why?" I finally asked. I should have asked him right off the bat.

"You said that you want to make something right," he said. "I do too. I know my canceling the road trip and sending you that letter screwed everything up between us."

"Things were already a little screwy," I said. "We got too close too quickly. You were still devastated. I was lonely. We were a disaster waiting to happen."

"So why not set it right? Call it a do-over."

My heart quivered before seemingly wedging itself in my throat again.

"Technically it can't be a do-*over*, since we never actually got around to doing it the first time," I pointed out. Pedantic, I know. And maybe even a little shitty.

"Good point," he said. "So call it a second chance at once in a lifetime."

Oh man, the tingles. He certainly did have a way with words.

"What, exactly, are we giving a second chance? Our friendship? The prospect of being more than friends? Because I don't think I want to go there again. We were deluded to think we could be anything more."

"Forget the labels," he said. "We had a great *relationship*. Wouldn't it be nice to reconnect to that? Plus think of the story we could tell," he tacked on.

Sooner or later, we always got back to the story. Perhaps he knew I wouldn't be able to resist that bait. Several premises flashed before me:

1. Boy meets girl. Boy and girl become friends. Boy gets divorced. Boy stomps on girl's heart. Girl shoots boy with laser gun and runs off with British new wave band.

2. Boy and girl go on road trip. Girl gets carsick. Boy leaves her on side of road to hitchhike. Girl gets picked up by sexiest man alive and they run off to Fiji to live happily ever after.

3. Boy and girl drive in car and argue for twelve hours straight about who made a better Darrin in *Bewitched*— Dick York or Dick Sargent.

"Or the games we could play," I said. "'Murder on the Pacific Coast Highway.'"

He laughed. "'I Spy a Shit-Ton of Dramamine,'" he countered.

My turn to laugh. "'Punch Buggy Hematoma,'" I said.

We both cackled.

The banter felt so good, so easy, reminiscent of when distance was measured only in physical miles. Even better than the Facebook exchange. And as if on a delayed reaction, his words hit me: *We had a great relationship.* His sincerity petrified me. How? How was it possible to have romantic feelings for someone you'd only been in a room with once in the last two and a half years, eleven months of those spent incommunicado?

It wasn't. The alleged romance wasn't real. "Merriweather and Moss" was a work of fiction.

My father had been a work of fiction too. Hell, the word *father* was a work of fiction in his case.

And, in hindsight, that had been the real heartbreak. In the case with Jon, I'd felt so foolish, so duped. I spent the first couple of months reeling from the humiliation as much as the disappointment, even though Kalvin, Hazel, and Gaia were the only ones in the know. I wore sunglasses everywhere I went, rain or shine, indoors or out. I went off the grid. Once that phase was over, I wrote like a fiend. Five thousand words a day for three months straight. Few days off. Two manuscripts completed, one of them being *Change at Jamaica.* Great for my career, lousy for my life.

Until one day I woke up and decided to go to the beach. And I sat and stared at the ocean for what seemed like hours. And then I stood up and said, out loud, "Enough." He was a guy, that's all.

But he was also my friend.

Still, I knew it was time to move on.

Why on earth would I put myself through the delusion and disappointment again? Sure, I missed Jonathan's friendship, but what if even that hadn't been real?

A road trip? A second chance? The two of us trapped in a car for days? No way. *No way.*

It was close to midnight, although only nine o'clock in Tacoma.

"I think it's a bad idea, Jon," I said. "It was the first time around too. Neither of us was thinking straight. In fact, maybe we should just leave well enough alone."

23

The deflation was palpable. "You're right," he said.

"You hurt me, you know. That letter just about crushed me." The words spewed out, traveled through the phone ether, and slapped him in the face.

He paused for a beat before answering, "I know." His tone was remorseful. "I've regretted it ever since."

I could feel another round of tears coming on. I was the one who'd extended the olive branch. So why did I just beat him with it?

"I should go," I said. "Thank you for listening rather than hanging up on me. I'm sorry I bothered you tonight."

"Sage, you have never been, nor will you ever be, a bother. Thank you for calling me," he said. "I'm really sorry about your father."

"Good night."

"Good night," he replied. "Sleep well."

"You too."

I tapped my phone to end the call, sucked in a deep breath, and exhaled forcefully.

Shit. So much for righting a wrong.

Again I clicked off the light and scrunched under the covers. While waiting for the sleep that I knew likely wouldn't come, I mentally replayed the entire conversation, almost verbatim.

Every time I closed my eyes I saw Jonathan's author photo, the one of him standing in front of the all-encompassing vista of Mount Rainier. He wore "author glasses"—thick, dark Clark Kent frames. Facial hair to compensate for his receding hairline. A crimson polo shirt. He looked more golfer than geek, blue-blooded than bookish, and he was certainly more pragmatic than academic. He preferred Adidas to Armani. He was tall, yes—towering, in fact, but girth replaced gangly. In fact, Jonathan Moss was as far from my type as one could be, if one was only judging books by their covers.

I slid out of bed and padded into the living room lit only by the streetlamp blotted by maple leaves fluttering in the nighttime breeze, casting a feathery glow across my bookcase. I didn't need light to find Jonathan's name on the shelf. His books aligned themselves next to mine at the top, centered, like buddies hanging out together.

My fingers delicately grazed across the spine of the complimentary advance copy of *Bleacher Seats*. The publisher had sent it, but Jon had inscribed it:

To Sage, with thanks for your kindness.

The ink had blotted when a tear dropped on the end of his signature upon my reading it the first time.

I tilted the book and let it bow forward as I removed it, flipped to the back cover, and studied Jonathan and the mountain behind him. Mount Rainier was a helluva hill to climb—not to mention that it wasn't so much a mountain as it was a volcano. Ready to blow at any moment.

A second chance.

No. Friggin'. Way.

CHAPTER FIVE

The following afternoon Gaia, perched in lotus position on the couch, wrapped herself in a Snuggie and clutched a box of tissues while I sat horizontally in the recliner, my feet draped over the arm. I brought chicken soup and enough garlic bread to repel the entire cast of *Twilight*. With the exception of Hazel and Kalvin, Gaia was the only person who knew the full story of what happened—or rather, what didn't happen—between Jonathan and me. Even my mom didn't know. Like the awesome big sister she is, Gaia had invited me over on countless lonely Saturday nights to bake and watch movies and hold me while I cried on her shoulder. She'd been my only outlet. In retrospect, it wasn't much different from the way we'd banded together after Dad left.

"OK, so this is an interesting turn of events," she said after learning about the previous night's call and Jon's idea. "And this was the first time you two have spoken in how long?"

"Months. Since our editor asked me to write a blurb for his book. And one Facebook exchange last week."

Jon and I shared the same acquisitions editor, Joel Forsythe, at Bellevue Pages, our publisher. Unbeknownst to Jon, Joel had e-mailed me the blurb request for Jon's latest novel, *Bleacher Seats*, not realizing that Jon and I were on the outs, much less that we had been friends in the first place. I knew why Joel had chosen me—Jon had told me that Joel wanted him to attract more female readers (*Funny, no one ever insists I attract more male readers—and believe me, I'd love to,* I'd complained in response). An endorsement from a bona fide "women's author" would supposedly help.

By then it had been only two months since the canceled trip and my telling Jon what he could do with the nonrefundable plane tickets I'd purchased. Two months since I'd hidden him on Facebook, deleted his texts, and written him out of my life after he'd released me from his. Two months since the end of morning and evening phone calls, sending each other a Song of the Day, watching the same movie from our respective couches while texting with each other. Just seeing his name in the subject heading of Joel's e-mail had kicked my heart back fifty yards after I'd pushed it so far up the field. (Jon would love the football metaphor.) I had considered making up a bogus excuse about having too much on my plate, but the truth was that Jonathan Moss was one of the best writers I knew, and the excerpts he'd shared with me while undergoing the drafting process were annoyingly brilliant. So I told Joel that I'd be honored to do it. With every turned page of the galley, the torrent of hurt and anger at Jonathan Moss the Guy whirlpooled with the reverence and love for Jonathan Moss the Writer, and the Writer won out. A year into our friendship, after reading a poignant short story he'd written, I'd messaged him: `Every time I read something you've written, I want to know you a little better.`

After reading *Bleacher Seats*, I felt as if I did. And I missed him horribly.

I'd copied Jon on the e-mail to Joel with my official endorsement:

No one I know captures the human condition better than Jonathan Moss. He is a reader's writer, putting words together in ways that are elegant and earnest, composed and crafted. Moss makes me want—no, *need*—to step up my game. Most encouraging of all is that he'll keep stepping up his own.

He had texted me about an hour later: I didn't know Joel asked you for a blurb. Thank you. I appreciate your taking the time, and the kind words.

You'll always be one of my favorite writers, I'd texted in reply.

And you'll always be one of mine.

You know that feeling of your heart being squeezed to the point where you think it will explode? That's what a simple text did to me. Looking back, I could have reopened the lines of communication, offered reconciliation along with the endorsement. I'd desperately wanted to. So why didn't I?

Because I'd remembered the unanswered letters I mailed my father during my teen years, filling him in on my school achievements and interests (highlighting that I aced math, hoping maybe that would win favor). I'd remembered the telephone messages I left on his answering machine that were never reciprocated. I'd remembered the Father's Day cards that were left unacknowledged.

Jonathan closed the door on me first. I wasn't about to open it and wait for him to walk through. Even if he did, I couldn't trust that he wouldn't walk right back out again.

Gaia sneezed, honked into her tissue, and sniffled, the tip of her nose rosy and sore. "Well, the fact that you're here means you're actually considering this trip, which makes you as crazy as he is."

"Not necessarily," I said. "But even if I were, then why is it crazy to want to make things right with someone who was once a close friend?"

"A close friend with whom you'd only been in an actual room together once two years ago. At a party. And his wife was there. And everyone was drunk."

"You have friendships with people who no longer live on the island that, if you saw tomorrow, would pick up as if not a day had passed since you last saw them."

"Sure. Friendships that began with face-to-face, personal human contact. Not some online correspondence. And what, exactly, do you want to make right?"

"It wasn't just a 'correspondence,'" I argued. "We were *friends*. We shared things. Told stories. You can achieve personal connection with words. In fact, I make a living at it. So does he." I crossed my arms in further defiance. "I miss my friend. There. I admit it. I want to go back to before we entertained the notion of being anything more."

"You can't go back, Sage," said Gaia. "You just can't. And considering that the whole purpose of the road trip was to explore the possibilities beyond friendship, I don't see how it's a good idea now. Come on, Sis, we've been through this. We agreed the timing was lousy. We agreed you were both swept up in foolish romantic notions. We agreed it had been an impulsive, unrealistic fantasy from the get-go."

Thing is, deep down I never believed it. Not when Jon's letter still echoed in the recesses of my heart during nights when I couldn't sleep: *I know we have an opportunity with this road trip that few people get: the chance to start our journey together from a place of absolute and enduring honesty.* How on earth could that have been a lie?

"You're right," I said. "It will always be awkward."

"So it's settled, then," she said.

"It was never unsettled," I replied.

"Trust me," she started, and sneezed. "You don't need this."

~

Ever since Hazel Scott and her husband, JT, relocated to Connecticut from Vermont so her kids could attend UConn and not have to pay the exorbitant out-of-state tuition and fees, she and I had been taking turns riding the Port Jefferson Ferry to and from Bridgeport at least twice a month to spend time together. Today we sat in Toast café in Port Jefferson with our buddy Kalvin, who was in town for an MFA panel discussion on the merits of horror as a genre, blissing out on Belgian waffles.

"So remember that road trip Mossy and I were supposed to take last year? Well, he suggested we try again this year," I announced.

"Dude! About freaking time!" said Hazel.

"Wait—you *knew*?"

"He floated the idea past me after that hilarious exchange you two had on my Macy's balloon thread," said Hazel.

Why should it surprise me? Jonathan and Hazel were almost as close as she and I were—in fact, had we lived in closer proximity, we'd probably all be renting a house together. Or so we joked. Kalvin rounded out our author foursome—he penned under the creepy name Alistair Willow and was contracted with Kent Books, the horror fiction imprint under the large umbrella of Mammoth Publishing, our parent company, which also housed the Bellevue Pages imprint. She, Kalvin, Jon, and I dubbed ourselves the Fantastic Four, although we couldn't quite agree on who should be whom other than insisting that Jonathan totally was the Thing, regardless of whether he actually wanted to be. Although how could our quartet ever be as tight again?

I eyed Kalvin. "And you?"

"Clueless," he said. "Although I did take note of that Thanksgiving parade balloon thread. Made me happy, and not just because it was funny."

"So what do you think?" I asked them.

"I encouraged him to ask you, and now that he has, I totally think you should do it," said Hazel.

"Why?" I asked.

"Because you both need to fix this shit," she said.

"I don't know if it can be fixed."

Hazel placed her fork on the table. "Sage, why do I feel like you and Mossy are this phenomenal love story that everyone missed?"

"It's like we came into the theater after the lights came on as the credits rolled," Kalvin added.

"There was no love story," I said. "Never. I got it wrong, OK? I thought we were . . . that we felt . . . I thought he wanted to be with me, and he didn't."

"He *did* want to be with you," said Hazel. "But he just couldn't handle it when he was going through his divorce. He had to unpack all that pain first. And then the one thing he was sure of, his friendship with you, was no longer certain because he suddenly didn't think of you as a friend, and he was terrified to lose you too—or worse, hurt you. So he did the only loving thing he could at the time."

"But he didn't just cancel the trip. He let *me* go. He let the friendship go. Everything. He killed it all."

"No, *you* did that. You freaked the fuck out and went nuclear on him. All he needed was a little time and space."

Kalvin nodded in agreement. "Sorry to be ganging up on you here, but it's true."

I pushed my plate away.

"I think you want to say yes to this trip, and I think it's because you want to see what will happen. And I think something will," said Hazel.

A pitter-patter of *Yes!* was instantly followed by a warning bark of *No!*

"And if something does, then what happens after that?" I asked.

"Then Merry Christmas and Happy New Year!" she said.

"No," I said. "No. No. No. The same problem we had before— namely, an expanse of landmass"—my arms outstretched—"will still be there. And you know he ain't leaving Tacoma, and you know I ain't leaving Long Island. No," I reiterated. "I'm not doing it. I can't. I just can't. Jon bailed on me three days before I was scheduled to fly to Phoenix last year; did you know that?"

"Wow," she said. "I didn't know that. Must have been too ashamed to tell me."

"So was I," I said.

Kalvin shook his head. "I swear, you and Jon are a Nora Ephron movie being directed by Ed Wood."

"Yes," I said. "Yes, we are."

After our meal and a walk around Port Jefferson village, Hazel and I said our good-byes to Kalvin, who took off up the street in search of his car. As she was about to board the ferry back to Connecticut, I clutched her arm. "Do you really think it's a good idea?" I asked.

She looked me square in the eye. "Sweetie, you know I love you and want you to be happy. Ditto for Moss. So I can't tell you whether you're making a mistake. I want you and Jon to patch things up, and I want you to do it while breathing the same air."

Hazel and Kalvin were also the only two to know about my dad dying.

"But you need to do what's best for you," she said. "I'll support you no matter what."

She hugged me tight and boarded the ferry, and I returned to the Beetle more confused than ever about what to do.

CHAPTER SIX

When I got home, I checked e-mails to find one from Kathleen, subject heading: *Memorial.* I opened it and read:

> Information regarding the memorial of
> Thomas C. Merriweather . . .
>
> Date: January 1, 2017
>
> Time: 3:00 p.m.
>
> Place: Golf Club of Sacramento
>
> Coffee and cake immediately following at the Merriweather residence.

Seriously? A formal invitation?
For a memorial?
On New Year's Day??
To his *daughter*???

Then I read the P.S. (a freaking P.S.!):

You are under no obligation to attend.

Sometimes I think "blood boiling" is more than a metaphor. I swore I heard mine bubbling as it rushed through my veins.

Obligation. That's all this e-mail was to her. She couldn't even pick up the phone. She made the memorial sound like an obligation too. Her obligation, that is.

And what about *his* obligation? He had been obligated to be a father to Gaia and me. But I'd never wanted obligation. I'd wanted a *dad.* Someone who looked forward to coming home from work so he could kiss me hello and help me with my homework and read stories to me at bedtime and teach me chords on the guitar or scales on the piano or beats on the drums.

I picked up the phone and called Gaia.

"Did you see this shit?" I asked when she answered.

"The e-mail about the memorial? Yeah."

"And you didn't call me?"

"Why should I call you? I figured you got it too," she said.

"Unbelievable," I said.

"What is?"

"That she would send us an e-mail rather than call us. That she would schedule a memorial for her husband on New Year's Day."

"Sage, this is Kathleen you're talking about. Why would you expect reasonable?"

She had a point. But still, why wasn't Gaia outraged?

"Are you going?" I asked.

"To what?"

Gaia's ignorance was starting to annoy me. "To the memorial!"

"Why on earth would I go to the memorial?"

She really didn't know? "Because Kathleen doesn't think we would. It would be glorious to see the look on her face if we showed up. Not to mention how much it would piss her off."

Gaia was silent for an extra beat. "That's not a good reason to go to someone's memorial. Even someone who treated you shittily."

Now I was downright pissed off at my sister. "I can't believe you're not siding with me on this."

"It's not a question of taking a side, Sis. It's just a lousy reason to spend a lot of money on something spiteful. I stopped having a relationship with Dad and Kathleen because I wanted less negativity in my life. You're proposing something full of negativity. Just let it go. Neither of them is worth it."

"Fine," I said, and brushed Gaia off the phone. Logged out of e-mail and tried to work on my latest manuscript to no avail. Stupid Kathleen. Stupid memorial. Stupid everything.

Later that night, I lay in bed alone and awake. My dead dad continued to rent space in my head. I couldn't stop writing different versions of the same scene—a chance for me to talk to him one more time. One version had him calling me out of the blue to apologize for the last thirtysome years and wish me well. Another had me calling him to tell him off. Yet another had me forgiving him but telling off Kathleen.

Not a single one was satisfying. Or possible.

Who the hell was she to control if or how or where we paid our respects and said good-bye? Who the hell was he to leave us behind like an old used couch?

I needed to go to Sacramento and this memorial for the sole reason that Kathleen probably wouldn't expect me to. I needed to confront Kathleen and tell her off once and for all. I needed to see what my father gave up life with Mom and Gaia and me for.

I wouldn't want to do it alone, though.

I glanced at the clock. Just after 2:00 a.m. Which meant that it was just after 11:00 p.m. in Tacoma. I rolled over, reached for my phone, activated the screen, and tapped the Facebook app, scrolling through the news feed, and found a status update from Jon:

```
Being an Arizona Cardinals fan has about
as much social payback as listening to
Coldplay.
```

I laughed quietly, fondly, reminiscently. And just as I was about to type: *You listen to Coldplay? Holy shit, you think you know a guy . . .* a notification from Messenger appeared.

```
Got a minute?
```

Goose bumps. As if he'd somehow *sensed* my presence.

Our hour-long conversations usually started with *Got a minute?* We'd disappear into each other's spaces for an hour full of rampant typing and laughter, and I'd go back to whatever I was doing feeling like I'd just taken an invigorating walk or shower, or watched a good TV show.

Was he trying to initiate that again? Or did he genuinely want to chat briefly? I had never needed to read into Jon's actions before, or mine, and I didn't like that I was doing so now.

```
Sure, I typed.
```

```
Not making this public until the contracts
are signed, but Joel gave me the green
light for the newest novel. You're the
first to know.
```

If a heart could smile—I mean physically morph its shape into that of the happy face—then mine just did. A soft one, without parting lips or showing teeth. One of satisfaction, a faintly smoldering ember in an otherwise snuffed-out flame. And as much as I would have liked to tell myself his good news was responsible for it, I knew the real reason: *You're the first to know.* I hadn't offered him the same courtesy regarding *Change at Jamaica*, although when I found out, I'd suppressed the urge to tell him.

```
That's fantastic news, Jon. I appreciate
your telling me first
```

I stared at the face of the phone, desperate to say more, to know more, to snap my fingers and erase the last eleven months. Desperate for it to be easy.

The heart-smile wrenched and twisted into a vise grip of regret.

I typed slowly and deliberated on whether to hit "Send": `I've missed you`, I tapped. Message sent.

Seconds later, Jon replied: `I've missed you too.`

`As a friend`, I quickly added, needing to reinstate that boundary.

```
I understand.
```

Shit.

I typed: `My dad is still dead.`

```
Sounds like he's haunting you, though.
```

```
I hate him.
```

```
He missed out on a beautiful daughter.
```

My eyes welled up. I wanted to type, *If you feel that way, then why did you let me go too?* But the words seemed too big for a small screen.

Instead, I typed: TWO beautiful daughters.

I'm sorry it hurts so much.

Had lunch with Kalvin and Hazel today.
They both think we should do the road
trip.

It was a sharp segue even for me, but I wanted off the subject of my father, despite having been the one to bring it up. I nervously waited for his reply.

And?

That's it? "And?"

And I think you paid them a commission
to endorse you.

Only if you say yes, followed by a winking emoji.

Shit, was that flirting? I wasn't ready for flirting. Or willing. Flirting equaled danger. It led to things like buying plane tickets and then losing a fortune after someone freaks out and changes his mind and . . . *Boundaries, dammit. Boundaries!*

Despite my impulse to avoid the rest of the conversation and hide under the covers, the screen indicated he had more to say, so I waited.

Seriously, Sage. No pressure. I'll
completely understand if you don't want
to do it.

I finally came clean not only to him but also to myself:

```
I do want to do it. That's precisely the
problem.

Why is it a problem?

Because things are different between us
now.
```

I exhaled a heavy sigh of frustration, wanting to exit from this conversation thread as well. Although, like the previous one, *you started it, dumbass*.

Jon's reply appeared:

```
Suppose we set some ground rules.
```

I decided to play along because it seemed more like a challenge than a negotiation. Whether I was challenging myself or him, I wasn't sure. Nevertheless, the defiant, competitive part of me couldn't resist. Like knowing the trap was set, but trying to steal the bait unscathed.

```
Fine.
```

I started:

```
RULE #1: THERE WILL BE NO FLIRTING OR
SEXUAL INNUENDO OF ANY KIND. NOT EVEN AS
A JOKE.
```

Seconds later, his response appeared.

```
Deal.
```

I continued:

```
RULE #2: WE SLEEP IN SEPARATE BEDS.
```

I was originally going to insist on separate *rooms*, but even though Jon had offered to foot the entire bill, I didn't feel right taking advantage of his generosity. That said, I was equally reluctant to invest in the trip given how much money I'd wound up losing the last time on canceled flights, nonreturnable Christmas gifts, and sexy pajamas that I'd returned to the store, tags still attached.

I added:

```
I RESERVE THE RIGHT TO REQUEST SEPARATE
ROOMS AT ANY TIME.
```

```
OK
```

OK??? Shit.

```
RULE #3: THERE WILL BE NO ALCOHOL. ARE YOU
GETTING MY DRIFT, MOSS? ALCOHOL LOWERS
INHIBITION AND THERE WILL BE NO LOWERING
OF INHIBITIONS.
WHY ARE YOU SHOUTING AT ME? he replied.
```

I resumed lowercase for the reply.

```
I'm serious, Jon. Not one Newcastle.
```

```
I promise I'll teetotal it the entire trip.
```

Was anything going to rattle him?

RULE #4: THERE WILL BE NO SEX.

My phone buzzed:

It's going to be a platonic event,
Merriweather.

He was being way too agreeable. But I had every intention of adhering to and enforcing these rules, and considered getting them notarized as well. I tried to think of a Rule Number Five but drew a blank. Meanwhile, my phone buzzed again.

Does this mean you're saying yes?

I stared at the phone screen, drawing long, hard breaths.
This is crazy. You're not thinking straight. You're sleep deprived. Grief deprived. Fucked in the head.

I think so.

Five seconds passed with no response. Not even the three flashing dots to indicate that he was in the middle of typing.
Ten seconds.
Twenty.
I was about to put my phone on the bedside table when it rang, practically jolting me off the bed.
"Hi, Jon," I said.
"I figured we should actually *talk* about this now. Are you sure you want to do this?"
"No. Yes. I think so."

"What changed your mind?"

"I'm going to Sacramento to see my father. His memorial, I mean. Kathleen is having one on New Year's Day, which is weird to me, but whatever."

Whoa—when did I make *that* decision? And yet, the moment I said it, I was fully committed to doing so.

"That's a big thing to do."

"I figured we could make it part of the road trip, if you didn't mind accompanying me."

"But what's your primary reason for taking the trip? To see me, or see your dad?"

The question squeezed me from both sides. "Why can't it be both?"

"Why do you want to see me?"

"Because . . ." I started, and fell short. Geez, we did so much better when we e-mailed each other. At least then I had time to sort out my thoughts and match them with the perfect word choices.

"I'm . . . looking for something," I said.

"What?"

"Me."

"I don't understand," he said.

Neither did I. "I always felt like I lost a part of me that I could never recover when my dad left. I think I lost something with you too. Maybe by taking this trip with you, I'll find it again."

"Why not take the trip with your sister?"

"Gaia wants no part of it. Besides, the road trip part could be what we originally intended before we introduced all the romantic possibilities: a chance for two friends who haven't seen each other in a long time to hang out, have a bunch of laughs, and deal with some shit together."

"You're sure?"

"I'm sure."

"OK," he said.

"OK," I echoed.

"Well, great. I'll be in touch with details and itinerary. I'll even make your plane reservations for you."

"Thanks," I said.

"I'm looking forward to seeing you."

"Me too." The clock now read 3:00 a.m. Yet another minute turned into an hour. "It's super late. I need to sleep."

"OK," he said.

"Good night, Moss."

"Good night, Merriweather."

I ended the call. And then I broke out into the shivers.

Holy freaking fuck, what have I done?

CHAPTER SEVEN

December 29

If you saw a chick dragging her ass through the jet bridge and into the terminal, laptop case and purse over her shoulder, clumsily cradling bulky layers of East Coast winter garments removed en route, that was me.

I arrived in Phoenix at night. In addition to Dramamine for airsickness, I'd taken a homeopathic equivalent of Xanax. As I exited the plane, nerves set in yet again, although somewhat dulled by the Xanax knockoff. Every step was one closer to Jonathan Moss. One year ago I'd played out different versions of this moment—the tearful embrace that would last for a good two minutes; the first kiss (also lasting two minutes); the Harlequin-version pick-me-up-and-spin-me-around-embrace-followed-by-the-passionate-kiss (the most unlikely and corniest of the three, but fun to fantasize). And in the months that followed our demise, I'd doubted whether we'd have any moment of communication again, let alone one that involved physically touching each other. That doubt had been even more crushing than the disappointment of the canceled trip.

What if this had all been nothing more than a fantasy, a story we'd made up? Because let's face it: Jonathan and I were used to living in worlds of our own construction and filling in our own details. And it was a hell of a lot easier to love someone from across the country when you saw only what was shown to you.

Gaia told me I was making a supersized mistake. Not just where Jon was concerned, but seeing Dad. Or, more specifically, what was left of Dad.

"Why do that to yourself?" she'd said when I told her. "It's not going to give you any clue as to *why* he left. All it's going to do is remind you *that* he left." Mom was pretty much in the same boat. I stubbornly insisted otherwise—having a clear picture of who he became would stop me from wondering what might have been.

As for Jon, Gaia simply said, "I think you're writing too many alternate endings in your head again. Real life plays out very differently."

"The whole point is to *stop* with the alternate endings in my head," I argued. Concerning both Dad and Jon. "Is that such a bad thing?"

It occurred to me that maybe Gaia and Mom were right as I rode the escalator down to baggage claim. Until I found him at the bottom—easy to spot, he was so freaking tall—grinning ear to ear, and the butterflies in my stomach started their own percussion session while my heart pounded in syncopation.

I had resolved to find superficial flaws in Jonathan Moss at every turn, my own shallowness be damned—anything to keep me from tripping over the platonic line and falling flat on my face again. So I took note of the receding hairline and the faded extra-large black T-shirt and saggy blue jeans and dirty sneakers and the Clark Kent glasses whose frames were too stark for his face and the mole on his neck I'd never noticed before. I even secretly inspected his fingernails. No chewed cuticles or bitten free edges, although they were sawed off due to his guitar playing, accompanied by callused fingertips. Beard neatly trimmed, although I preferred clean-shaven.

Plus, you know, the height discrepancy.

You know when you meet a celebrity for the first time in person, and your eyes have to adjust to seeing them three-dimensionally rather than two? I think that's part of being starstruck. It's an ironically surreal moment to discover that they are, in fact, real. They breathe. They eat. They're naked underneath their clothes just like the rest of us. I knew it was going to be this way. Even a year ago, I knew it was going to be weird. *I can't wait to find out what he smells like,* I used to think. It had always bothered me that I didn't have any sensory knowledge of him. What if his pheromones didn't get along with my pheromones? What if he had chronic halitosis? What if he smelled like cheese? Or gas? Or whatever Tacoma smells like?

Then again, what if he smelled so good I'd never be able to keep away?

He held a sign that read "SAGE 'SQUEAKY' MERRIWEATHER," which drew a swift-albeit-tired laugh from me. He'd dubbed me Squeaky following a FaceTime chat a year and a half ago when he witnessed my out-of-control, beverage-out-the-nose, tears-streaming-down-the-face laugh for the first time. The kind that makes you cry and squeak and snort and hold your side from the stitch and literally fall over and pray you don't wet your pants. It was a crowning achievement for him to get me to laugh like that, he'd said. One of the highlights of our friendship.

Jon fanned his arms open like wings, waiting to fold me into them. I dropped the balled-up jacket and cardigan, removed the shoulder bags and placed them at our feet, and stepped in to hug him.

The first thing I did was inhale. He smelled like fabric softener. I'm not sure whether this relieved or disappointed me.

But God, he was warm. Like stepping into a fur coat.

Shit. Being in Jonathan's arms felt every bit as good as I used to imagine it would.

I pulled myself away as we made bespectacled eye contact and a goofy grin took over my face without my consent.

He had slimmed down quite a bit in the past year—about thirty pounds, and that sight alone was jarring—but he still had enough of a middle-aged spread to cushion me. He'd once asked me early into our friendship if his girth was a sexual turnoff.

Would you ever sleep with someone as heavy as I am? he'd asked.

Depends on his taste in music, I'd replied.

He'd laughed and brushed it off.

At the time I'd wondered if he was feeling me out, so to speak, but in hindsight I think he was wrestling with something much closer to home, namely his own self-worth, and possibly a marital issue as well. And I wished I hadn't been so flip about it. I was simply trying to enforce the boundaries I'd set with my married male friends.

"How was the flight?" he asked as we walked to the baggage carousel, slinging my laptop case strap over his shoulder and carrying my coat. I paid attention to his gait—no slouch or limp, so nothing to critique there.

"Crowded. Delayed. Turbulent," I replied. Forget the fear factor; flying just sucks in general—being jammed in like sardines, checking luggage (and given how I pack, I *always* have to check luggage), crying babies, bad food. Flying during the winter holidays is its own form of hell. I couldn't help but wonder if the turbulence was foreshadowing.

"That sucks. I'm sorry to hear it. How are you feeling?"

"Tired. And a little wonky."

This is awkward.

Our conversation, demeanor, interacting—everything was simultaneously comfortable and stilted, familiar and foreign. We were walking and talking like buddies, but the reality was that we had reverted to strangers. Theoretically we had plenty to catch up on. But quantity wasn't my concern. It was whether we'd forgotten *how* to talk to each other.

"You up for grabbing dinner, or do you want to go straight to the hotel and hit the hay—just you, I meant," he quickly tacked on after I shot him a Rule-Number-Four-enforcing glare.

"I kind of want something to eat, but I don't really have an appetite. I'm definitely not up for going out anywhere."

"How about we get a couple of slices of pizza, take them to your room, and just chill out watching mindless TV until you're ready to crash," he said.

"That might be ten minutes after we get there," I said.

"That's OK. I remembered to expect you not to be in top form tonight. Say the word and I'll go at any time."

"I appreciate your understanding," I said.

Both suitcases appeared on the baggage carousel, slowly riding toward us, looking as exhausted from the flight as I was. (I know what you're thinking: *Two suitcases for a four-day trip?* What can I say? I'm high maintenance. I fill an overnight bag just with hair products—a side effect of working in the salon industry. I anticipate weather conditions, social conditions, and sleeping conditions. I always bring more underwear than I need. It was a wonder I packed only two pairs of shoes, not including the ones I was wearing.) Jon grabbed the larger suitcase as I seized the smaller, and we headed for the sliding glass doors to zigzag between parked cabs and black Suburbans with tinted windows.

"The hotel is about a mile away," he said. "It's your basic Comfort Inn, but it's one of the newer ones. Workout room, pool, hot tub, room service . . ."

We were killing each other with cordiality. I had to put a stop to it.

"Cool. I'm throwing a party after you leave," I said.

He laughed. Mission accomplished.

"Also, pizza in Arizona is about as bad as you think it is."

"It's OK. I doubt I'm really going to taste it. I've been chewing gum and ginger snaps for the last eight hours."

"Well, here she is," said Jon as we arrived at his car—a bright-blue Ford Expedition. I had teased him relentlessly when he purchased it last September, telling him, *Friends don't let friends drive Fords.* "Meet Penelope."

"Pleased to meet you," I said, jiggling the door handle in a mock handshake.

He opened the back and placed the bags inside; his own would be joining them early tomorrow. After he gallantly opened the door for me and I clumsily climbed in (still had new-car smell), he trotted around to his side, stepped in, and turned the ignition key.

Alone. Together. First time ever.

Of course I'd been alone in cars with guys before. But never before had I felt as if the world stopped just to give me a moment to breathe. As if all bustle and activity and war and politics ceased, and some benign force said, *It's all yours from here on out. Take hold.*

All we'd done was close the doors. But sitting inches away from each other, after a two-year virtual relationship, was like stepping into a new dimension. Like Charlie Bucket in the Wonkavator. Life was about to change.

I glanced at Jon nervously. Was he feeling it?

He returned my glance and smiled. "I'm glad you're finally here," he said.

I smiled too, convinced he could hear my heart pounding.

He started the car and backed out of the parking space. "So, you had a good Christmas?" he asked as he followed the "Exit" signs. I couldn't help but wonder if he was genuinely interested or afraid of awkward silence setting in.

"Yeah, it was nice," I replied. "Quiet. My sister and brother-in-law and niece, my mom, and me in the Sag. Some extended family the following day. You?"

"Really nice. I'm ready to go home, though. I always get a little antsy after a few days."

"Too much family, or too few mountains?"

"Too much Arizona," he said. I somehow understood. One year ago, the chance to see where Jon grew up would've been akin to taking a tour, finally getting a chance to connect the images from his novels to the real-life artifact. Beyond landmarks and nostalgia, it was about seeing those social constructs that helped shape and mold and define who he had become. And anything that made Jonathan Moss more real and less a screenshot was a good thing. I wondered if it would or could still be that way. Or, would seeing where he grew up shed some light on my own childhood, when my dad was still in the picture? After all, reading someone else's story almost always makes us "read" our own. And yet I wasn't sure I wanted to go back there. Reliving the good moments ultimately led to reliving the big bad one too.

Then again, why attach so much drama to it? If Jon wanted to show me his old stomping grounds, so be it. Sometimes a house is just a house, a school is just a school, and a memory is just a memory.

He pulled into a shopping center across the street from the Comfort Inn and bought three slices of pizza and two Cokes to go. I bought a bottle of water. We then drove across the street, and I checked in while Jon parked and retrieved my bags for me. We entered the room—and if you're wondering what it's like to enter a bedroom with a guy you've known for two years but never smelled until a half hour ago, I'll tell you: it's beyond weird. But it was also titillating. And I knew this juxtaposition was going to appear in every scenario for the next twenty-four hours.

Two queen-sized beds with a small table and two chairs in the far corner. I turned toward him and cocked an eyebrow.

"I got the double just in case, but I wasn't planning to stay tonight."

"OK."

A pang of disappointment pulsed in my chest. *Shit.* Which was more disappointing—that he wasn't staying? Or seeing the reality of the two beds in adherence to the rules I'd set in place?

Oh my God, Jonathan Moss and I are in a hotel room in Phoenix, Arizona. Together. Two days before New Year's Eve.

It was downright surreal. Never mind that he wasn't staying or that I felt like crap on a Triscuit or that everything so far had gone according to plan, if not the way I'd scripted it in my head. Here was a guy to whom, up until this year, I'd felt closer than any man I'd dated or friend I'd physically hung out with on a regular basis. Here, in the flesh, standing next to the suitcase with my underwear in it. I could take two steps forward and hug him if I wanted to. Could arm-wrestle him. Could simply pinch him to prove he was standing there. As if I'd been in solitary confinement the last year and was reassimilating to human interaction.

I placed the food on the table while Jon turned on the TV. Next, I went to the bathroom, splashed some water on my face, toweled off, and returned. He found *South Park* after channel surfing and set a place for me at the table.

"This OK?" he asked, pointing to the TV. I nodded and sat down, feeling uncharacteristically shy. He'd already finished most of one slice and a Coke. I took a few bites and left the rest, each bite having lodged itself in my esophagus before thudding into the pit of my stomach.

"That bad?" he asked.

I shook my head. "I don't eat well on days I fly. My system gets worked up in such a frenzy from all the stress and anxiety." *And because I'm in freaking Arizona with you in a Comfort Inn with two beds on a road trip to visit my dead father.* As an afterthought, I added, "Although yeah, Arizona pizza does kind of taste like what I imagine the bottom of a shoe would taste like."

"I was going to compare it to the stuff that comes out when you change the oil in your car, but OK."

Was it going to be like this the entire trip? All small talk and jokes? Was that enough? Wasn't this what it was supposed to be, the way friends are supposed to be? Would I have been analyzing and question-ing every minute detail if I were on a road trip with any other friend?

I stood up and stretched, unsuccessfully stifling a never-ending yawn. Jon stood up as well. "I should go. You must be exhausted."

"You can stay and watch another episode if you want," I said, chased by a second yawn. Maybe I was getting used to his physical presence. Or maybe I didn't want to be alone in a place so new to me. Or maybe . . .

"OK," Jon said, his face slightly flushed. His eager acceptance made me blush as I tried to conceal my gratitude and unexpected delight. He returned to his seat while I relocated to the bed and propped the pillows up. Despite his conscious effort to not even peripherally glance in my direction, I couldn't help but feel his laser eyes boring a hole into me. We watched a second *South Park* episode and my eyes grew heavier with every bleeped expletive from Cartman. It was almost nine thirty. Eleven thirty, New York time. Before the end credits, I succumbed to the weight of slumber and closed my eyes.

I faintly heard Jon flick off the TV with the remote and, moments later, say in a tender voice, "I'm going to let you get some rest now."

"OK," I murmured.

"Call if you need anything. My parents don't live far—about five miles."

I opened my eyes in a squint to watch him clutch his wallet and keys from the table and shove them into his front pocket. I laid the pillows flat, crawled under the covers, and drew them to my neck, closing my eyes again while he collected the uneaten pizza and other trash and dumped it all into the wastebasket. When I opened my eyes one more time he was at my side, hovering, and for a second I thought he was going to bend down to kiss me good night. He looked like a tower of Jenga blocks, liable to topple over me at any second. My body was too tuckered out to escape from the path of his fall. Or maybe it wanted to catch him. But all he did was reach out to turn off the light for me. Had I not been so tired, I might have been bummed out. Then again, maybe I would have pulled away.

"Sleep well, Sage. See you in the morning."

"Is it always going to be this awkward?" I asked in a sleepy slur.

"It'll get better," he replied. "Welcome to Arizona."

"Good night, Moss."

"Good night, Merriweather."

He turned out the light and closed the door gently behind him. I desperately wished for him to come back.

Chapter Eight

December 30

At 7:55 a.m., to my surprise, I was actually showered, dressed, packed, and ready for Jon. *Awake*, however, was a matter of subjectivity. Although, the two-hour difference worked in my favor this morning.

Minutes later, the door knock in rhythmic rap signaled Jon's arrival, and I opened it to find him fresh and alert, dressed in jeans and a royal-blue T-shirt that read "Shakespeare was fucked," wearing a nervous grin that matched my own.

"Top o' the mornin' to ya," he said with exaggerated perkiness and a two-fingered salute. "How'd you sleep?"

"Like a rock. You?"

"Very well. I even worked out this morning."

I remembered that he'd started working out shortly after he and Shannon separated, and I'd packed workout clothes thinking maybe I would join him one morning. But he was usually up at five—or, at least, he used to be. It hit me that I no longer knew his routines and habits. They might have changed. On one hand, it bothered me that I had to get to know such details all over again. On the other hand, seeing them more organically, without textual commentary, was a dynamic whose importance, up until now, I'd taken for granted.

"Room's paid for, so we can just skadoodle out of here," he said.

Top o' the mornin'? Skadoodle? Jon wasn't usually this cheeseball. What the hell kind of protein powder did he put in his postworkout smoothie?

Together we lugged my stuff to the lobby; Penelope was parked in front of the entrance. I stepped outside expecting the Arizona air to be warm, but it was still crisp and chilly. Jon set the suitcases next to a duffel bag and a laptop case in the back of the SUV.

"That's all you brought?" I asked, pointing to his belongings.

"I'm a guy," he said, as if this were new information. "Plus, I've been in Arizona and along the West Coast all week. All T-shirt weather. And I don't have a hair routine." He tousled the remaining hair on his scalp.

I giggled at his self-deprecation. "I figured you would have brought your guitar."

"Don't really like to play in front of the family. Or anyone else, for that matter."

"You played for me," I reminded him. "Via FaceTime."

"Yes, and it terrified me."

"I didn't write a review for *Billboard*."

"I still wanted to get it right for you."

I'd confessed early into our friendship that I had a thing for guitar players. Clichéd, I know, but it was true. Give me your Eric Claptons, your Jimi Hendrixes, your Carlos Santanas. Even your John Mayers if you could keep their damn mouths shut when they weren't singing. I've been a piano player since I was eight, so I had proposed that I switch to drums and we get Kalvin to learn bass (he could pass for a brooding bass player) and Hazel for vocals (she played a mean kazoo, plus she had that Stevie Nicks vibe about her), and thus do a Battle of the Bands with Stephen King's Rock Bottom Remainders. *We'll call ourselves the Hacks,* said Jon on a Facebook thread. *Or the Mammoth Mofos.*

I climbed into Penelope and spotted two coffee cups between the bucket seats, one presumably for me. He must have forgotten that I didn't care for Starbucks coffee. Or had I ever told him? Were these the kinds of things we would have had to negotiate one year ago?

The caffeine did the trick. With every sip I was more awake.

Jon started putting his hands to his pockets, dashing left and right. "Oh, goddammit," he said.

"What?"

"I left my phone at my parents' house. I'm sorry."

"For what?" I asked.

"We have to go back and get it."

"What's wrong with that?" I said before the thought sank in: *Going back to Jonathan's parents' house. Where Jonathan's parents are. As in, meeting them. Like girlfriends do.*

Oh," I said. He understood. "Maybe I'll just wait in the car."

"I'll make it quick."

Last year he'd wanted me to meet his parents as well as show me around his neighborhood. I wanted it too. But last year was different. This year neither of us even mentioned it.

We pulled out of the hotel, drove up the street, and cut through a residential neighborhood. The houses were a mix of modern and Spanish-style, with brown-tipped grass lawns and cacti in place of azalea or hydrangea bushes out front. Odd to see Christmas lights and Santa sleighs on roofs in a state where snow had to be manufactured.

Jon pointed to a row of homes. "None of these were here when I was a kid. A lot of new neighborhoods and shopping centers. The entire town grew up after I did."

The metaphor wasn't lost on me—a place of such historical and emotional connection, simultaneously familiar and foreign.

"So why did you stay with your parents?" I asked.

"Free room and board," he replied. "Wouldn't you?"

I nodded. "Is your old bedroom like a shrine to your adolescence?"

"It's my dad's office now."

"So where did you sleep?"

"They turned my brother's room into a guest room."

"That must be strange," I said.

"A little," he said.

"What's it like being here when you come back to visit?"

"It's a peculiar kind of nostalgia. Like being in the twilight zone or a time warp. The house smells the same as when I was a kid. But my parents have repainted and upgraded and changed things around. And they're the same, but older versions of themselves. No complaints, though."

My mother kept the house she and my father bought when they got married until Gaia and I graduated high school—she'd thought it was important to keep us in the same school district and neighborhood so we could lean on our friends and teachers for support. I didn't fully appreciate the sacrifice she made until I was well on my own. It must have been difficult to live in that house with its memories, even though she made decorating changes—a painted room, a new slipcover for the couch, more plants—whenever she could scrape up enough pennies. After we went to college, she sold the house, took the equity, and purchased a piece of land in Sag Harbor, and, with what I later learned was an inheritance from her uncle, was able to build the house she lives in now. And although I never lived there, it felt more like home than the house Gaia and I had grown up in. Maybe it was because the memories no longer included the shadow of my father. Or maybe Mom just had good mojo.

We pulled into the driveway of a ranch-style home painted dark red with pristine white shutters. Neatly trimmed bushes lined up in the front, accented with colorful desert flowers. Jon pulled into the recently repaved asphalt driveway and killed the ignition.

"Be right back," he said as he unbuckled his seat belt and opened the door.

I suddenly wondered if he really was trying to spare me from the meet-the-parents moment, or if maybe he didn't want me to see his childhood home and meet his parents for reasons that had nothing to do with relationship status. What if he was ashamed of them? Or me?

And suddenly, the idea of him abandoning me in the car felt off-putting. I unbuckled my seat belt and opened the passenger door.

He turned around. "What are you doing?" he asked.

"I changed my mind," I said.

"You what?"

"I want to meet your parents."

As if on cue, the front door opened and a grinning elderly couple emerged. His mom, from whom Jon had inherited his eyes and smile, sported a white-haired bob that tucked under her ears, and she was dressed in capris and flip-flops, while his dad, from whom Jon inherited his receding hairline, wore carpenter shorts (on December 30!) and sneakers. Both wore faded Arizona Cardinals T-shirts. Had I not known they were in their midseventies, I would have guessed them to be ten years younger.

"Oh, great," he muttered.

"What?" I asked.

"They're going to invite us in. We'll never get out."

"So?" I said. "Why is that so awful?"

Before he could answer, his mom called out, "You changed your mind!"

"I left my phone here."

She was undeterred. "Well, come on in," she said. "Both of you."

Jon looked at me. "You're OK with this?" he mouthed.

"It's fine," I replied, making sure his parents were out of earshot. "I mean, sure, we haven't interacted outside of a computer in, like, never, but it'll be nice. I always get this terrified."

We shared a smile. "They're not crackpots, despite the fact that they live in Arizona."

"I heard that," said Mrs. Moss.

"Busted," I said.

We followed them up the walk, the net of butterflies letting loose inside me once more.

Jon's dad opened the door, and then he and Jon's mom stepped aside to allow us in as they greeted us and welcomed me.

"This is the famous Sage Merriweather," said Jon to his parents. To me, he said, "Meet the famous Marlene and Michael Moss. Mom's read all your books."

The revelation that the Mosses were already invested in me smacked me upside the head. At what point had Jon first mentioned me to them, and in what capacity? Sure, I'd mentioned Jon in conversation with my mom, and touted him as an author. But no more than Hazel or Kalvin or anyone else who was important to me.

I should have been weirded out. I *was* weirded out. At first. But a kind of affirmation settled in. As if I'd been recommended and initiated into a special club. One that invites you to take off your shoes the moment you enter, and not for the sake of clean floors.

"I could do without all the profanity, but I tell Jonnie that too," said his mother.

Jonathan turned crimson.

"I appreciate the support," I said. "And I'll try to cut down on the swearing for the next one. Just for you."

"So nice to finally meet you, Sage," said Mrs. Moss. "Have you eaten breakfast yet?"

The "finally" was not lost on me either. What, specifically, had Jon told them about me? I remembered the progression of referring to him as "my author friend" to "my friend" to "my good friend" whenever I mentioned him to Mom or Gaia. And even though he'd been demoted to "my former friend" in the last eleven months, prior to the day after Thanksgiving I'd never referred to him as such out loud. I imagined the possible identifiers from Jon: *Sage, the woman who lives on the other side of the country whom I've only met once; Sage, my friend whom I thought might be more than a friend who then turned out to be no friend at all and now wants to be friends again; Sage, my hairstylist-turned-author-turned-batshit-crazy friend who stopped speaking to me. (Come to think of it, she was always batshit crazy.)*

Thing is, Jon was never that wordy.

I answered Mrs. Moss's question with a no, and they invited me into the kitchen, where serving dishes of eggs and bacon and toast awaited us at an oval dark-wood table. As if they'd been expecting us. Maybe they'd hid his phone.

"I assumed you already ate," I said to Jon.

He nodded. "I had a slice of toast."

"Unacceptable," said Mrs. Moss. "You've got a long drive, and the less you eat at those fast-food places, the better."

As his mom fixed plates for each of us, Jon rolled his eyes, knowing he was beat, and joined me at the table. His father sat at the opposite end, a tablet resting on the table displaying a *New York Times* article waiting to be finished. A picture of Jon and me coming over for Sunday dinners and birthday parties and holiday barbecues flashed in front of me, and I was struck by how ordinary it felt. Not in the mundane sense, but as simple as spending time with my own family. I'd never experienced anything like that with a boyfriend, and I'm not sure if that was because I was trying too hard to win favor with those parents because the stakes were supposedly so high or because they'd all known I wasn't right for their sons.

I had to remind myself that the picture, albeit pretty, was nothing more than a scene conjured in the same imagination that wrote novels and was master of the what-if. For one thing, even though the scene had streaks of boyfriend-girlfriend all over it, I had no intention of making that a reality. Second, Jon loved his parents and siblings and visited at least once or twice a year, but Phoenix felt to him the way Bedford Falls felt to George Bailey in *It's a Wonderful Life*—stifling, although it was far from a small town. Even if we had become a couple, we certainly wouldn't have been putting down roots here. He once told me that he felt more at home in Tacoma than any other place he'd lived. Like he'd been misplaced at birth. I used to secretly hope that he'd feel differently once he visited Long Island, but it was a doomed hope. Even then I knew it was.

"So tell us about your latest book, Sage," said Mrs. Moss.

"I told you," said Jon. "She doesn't talk about works in progress."

When did he tell her that?

"I thought moms would get special treatment," she replied.

"*Her* mom, maybe," he retorted.

Was she that way with all Jon's friends? Was she the type of woman who thought of herself as a mom to everyone? Regardless, I had to fight off how good the idea of it felt.

"I'm sorry, Mrs. Moss," I said. "I just can't. Too superstitious, I guess."

She didn't seem hurt. "Marlene, please. All right, then tell us something else about you."

"What do you already know?" I asked, the question loaded with curiosity.

Before she could respond, Jon interjected with, "We gotta go, Mom." He sounded like a teenager rather than a forty-five-year-old. "Full itinerary." He still didn't have his phone.

"Don't you want to show her the house?" she asked.

Jon glared at his mother before turning to me. "OK, fine," said Jon.

We ate quickly, excused ourselves from the table, and took our empty plates to the sink. "What is your problem?" I asked under my breath while I helped him wash and dry the plates. "They're being nice."

"I don't want them treating you as if you're my girlfriend."

For some reason this irked me, despite my laying down the ground rules specifically stating that we were not to carry on as anything beyond friends. "Then why did you even mention me to them?"

"Why would I take an eight-hundred-mile road trip and not mention that I was traveling with someone?"

"I guess I was thrown by them saying it was nice to finally meet me. Like they'd been expecting me. Plus your mom has read my books."

"You were important to me. They knew that. I just . . . it hit me, that's all."

Were?

"What hit you?"

Before he could answer, Jon's mom came to the sink and took over, prompting him to give me the dime tour of the house in which he'd spent the first eighteen years of his life. The living room, where the family opened presents every Christmas and invited the neighbors over for carols and cocoa. The dining room, where Thanksgiving dinners took place, namely the one when Jon threw a turkey bone at his younger brother and it ricocheted off the chandelier and plopped into the mashed potatoes.

It occurred to me that I knew so many of his stories. And that both pleased and pained me.

Almost every room was sparsely furnished and neutrally decorated, but loaded with built-in shelves crammed with books and photos of children and grandchildren from various stages of life. He led me down the hallway, past the guest room formerly belonging to his brother, to the last room on the left.

"Here you go," he said. "My old room. You can probably still smell the dirty socks."

I scanned corner to corner, imagining what the umber-hued paint had covered up, what had previously occupied the spaces that a glass-topped computer desk and Ikea bookshelves and filing cabinets now occupied, what I would find if I opened the closet door.

"If these walls could talk . . ." I started.

"They'd say, 'Wow, that was one fucked-up kid.'"

"Come on," I said.

"That and 'No boy should use that much mousse. Even in the eighties.' Here," said Jon as he pulled out a thick binder with yellowed sticky pages covered in acetate. "I'm being preemptive. If I don't show them to you now, my mom will just drag you back in and show you herself." We sank into the squishy, outworn love seat opposite the desk (a relic from his childhood living room, I correctly guessed), and the feeling was not unlike cuddling up with an oversized fuzzy bear.

One that sent little heat flares up my spine and through my nerve endings with every physical contact.

Our legs brushed against each other with nowhere else to go as he propped the book on my lap, and the moment I opened the first page, I was transported back to 1970. A youthful, glowing Marlene Moss, with iron-straight flaxen hair and bell-bottoms and a gingham blouse, cradled infant Jonathan as she and a strapping black-bearded Michael Moss adoringly fawned over him. Next to that photo was months-old baby Jonathan, bright-eyed and fair-skinned and toothless, smiling.

I awwwed as I placed my hand on my chest. "Look at you," I said, my heart swelling with every Kodak moment. I momentarily switched my view to adult Jon, and he seemed content.

"I was cheek-pinchingly cute," he said. "And then I hit puberty."

"At least you had twelve good years," I said.

"Eight," he said. We laughed.

I eagerly flipped the pages and the narrative of Jon's childhood formed in faded color photos, some Polaroid, some Instamatic, some matted with white borders—Christmas mornings in footie pajamas showing off *Six Million Dollar Man* action figures and Big Wheels and Superman bedsheets; birthday parties with classmates—all sporting bowl cuts and bangs—and homemade cakes and streamers and party hats; elementary school portraits with clip-on ties and later polo shirts and Shaun Cassidy feathered hair; summer vacations at Disneyland and Six Flags and San Diego; Mickey Mouse ears and Fonzie T-shirts and oversized Dodgers baseball caps; long-lost pets—dachshund dogs and tabby cats and a hamster named Frank and a turtle named, aptly, Turtle.

Jon touched one of the photos with his thumb, as if stroking the dog's back. "I loved that dog. Cried for a week when he died."

"I don't recall you mentioning that one. What was his name?"

"Howard."

"Howard?"

"What can I say? We were *Happy Days* fans. He came close to being named Potsie. We gave that name to the cat instead. And she was a girl."

I cracked up.

With every turned page and comment and filling in of names and dates and places, the scents of musty paper and home cooking and air freshener swirling about us, you wouldn't have guessed we hadn't been in a room together in two years, or that we'd imploded just twelve months ago. What would have happened had we gone through with this road trip the first time around? Would we have been poring over photo albums? Or would I have been on the first plane back to LaGuardia before breakfast was over?

Jon viewed every page with equal parts nostalgia and repose. "I haven't looked at these albums in so long."

I pointed to a little boy and girl. "That's your brother and sister?"

"Yep. Mikey and Heather. We're all a year apart."

That I knew. I also knew that they still lived in Arizona, within a twenty-five-mile radius of their parents, who were active grandparents.

"You miss them?" I asked.

"My sibs? Yeah, it's always good to see them. Thanks to Facebook we keep in touch just about every day and I know what's going on in their lives, but it's not the same, you know?"

I couldn't imagine being a plane ride away from Gaia or my mom. And Erika and I took monthly shopping trips or after-school ice-cream jaunts. At twelve years old, she was already swearing me to secrecy about boys she liked. To lose that precious time would be devastating.

"We were really close as kids and teenagers," he said. "But after I went away to college and they got married and started families at the same time I was advancing my career and on the road a lot, we sort of diverged. I didn't relate to parenthood, and they didn't relate to journalism."

I nodded in recognition. "I think my mother was dumbfounded when I became a hairstylist. She wanted me to be an art therapist. She nearly had a coronary when I turned down a scholarship to Pratt. The truth was that I never thought I was good enough for a school like Pratt. All that raw talent there overwhelmed me. I had to work for every paintbrush stroke and pencil line. Cosmetology was different—it was more a playful and social art. And I later argued that as a stylist I was practicing a different kind of therapy."

"In what way?"

"There's something about touch that opens many people up. For the haggard mom, it was those few minutes of pampering. For the nurse practitioner, it was the opportunity to let someone else do the listening. For the teacher, it was like recess without the gaggle of kids. I watched them transform from the moment they sat in my chair to the moment they left. Their frown lines softened. Their eyes widened. Their skin glowed. They walked out feeling better about themselves and the world than when they walked in."

"Maybe it was just you," he said.

I blushed and averted the warmth emanating from him as well as the comment. "Plus, you know, novel fodder for me, although I didn't know it at the time. So many stories. And I think my clients taught me something about relationships."

"What, specifically?"

"That they're all fucked up," I said with a laugh. "But there's great comedy in the absurdity. And most of the fucked-up-ness comes from that absurdity."

He eyed me with fascination and inquisitiveness, as if to say, *That explains a lot.*

"Oddballs, we are," he said, and we high-fived. It was as if for the first time since I arrived, we'd forgotten to be deliberate. The spontaneity of such a simple gesture was like the loosening of a grip. An exhale. He turned solemn, however. "I especially miss being a part of my nieces' and nephews' lives. They don't really know me, and that hurts. I'm not sure what to do about it."

"You've never considered moving back?"

He shook his head vigorously. "Too hot," he said. "And arid. And they've got a shitty basketball team."

The comment drew another laugh from me. "Well," I said, "it's up to you to be present in their lives in other ways."

"How?"

"Snail mail, for starters. Send them cards, and not just on their birthdays. Text them pictures of yourself in your favorite places. Tell them stories. They'll reciprocate."

His eyes lingered on me as he absorbed my suggestions, and a soft smile appeared. "That's good advice," he said.

It would have been so easy to lean in—just mere inches—and kiss him. I could almost feel an invisible hand pushing me toward him. But I sat back and flipped to the next page.

I tried to imagine myself living in Phoenix. Or Tacoma. Or any place that wasn't Long Island. I tried to imagine waking up to a vista of palm trees or cacti or mountains, but I just couldn't see it. And it further compounded what I had ultimately concluded after Jon let me go: that even if we had taken the road trip the first time around and grew even closer, we wouldn't have been able to make it work. That the distance was too great. Sure, stories and cards were enough for a preteen niece or an eight-year-old nephew, but what chance did a romance have? When I caught myself imagining waking up in Jonathan's arms, I put a stop to it and focused on the last page of pictures.

When I closed the album and headed back to the kitchen, Jon behind me, I lingered to view the portraits in the hallway. Rows of prom and wedding and graduation photos. You know how in the movie *Pleasantville* when the words appeared on the pages of the books as Bud told his classmates their stories? I had already known Jon's stories about growing up in this suburb, but seeing the photographic evidence filled the pages in, breathed life into them, and somehow made the memories my own. And I wanted to read more.

I turned to face him, standing so close I could feel his breath on my neck as a microscopic mountain range of goose bumps spread down my arms. Was it *him*, or the newness of the sensual interaction with him? Was it just being in a narrow hallway with a guy after spending the morning in his childhood house, with his parents and photo albums and memories? Could that level of intimacy be achieved with some random stranger who showed me his home and his scrapbooks?

"You really did use a lot of mousse," I said as I observed his high school graduation portrait.

"I single-handedly kept Paul Mitchell in business." He stroked the remainder of hair atop his head. "Probably why I have so little now."

We reached the kitchen, and once again Jon informed his parents that it was time to go.

His mom handed him his phone. "Found it on the bedside table," she said.

"Thank you," he said.

"The Exxon off the interstate has gas at two-fifteen a gallon," said his dad.

"Thanks," said Jon. "I told you that I gassed up last night, remember? We're good to go."

"Ah, right." Mr. Moss hugged his son good-bye. His mother pulled him to her next. Then, to my surprise, she hugged me and said, "You're welcome here anytime, Sage." With a nudge in her son's direction, she added, "Bring him if you have to."

"Thank you," I said. "That's very nice of you." I hadn't expected to be pulled so deeply into her warmth, her inclusion, her acceptance. I hadn't expected to want to call any woman other than my own mother *Mom*. I hadn't expected to know Jon in such intimate ways so soon into our trip. I hadn't expected to wish Jon's father were mine. The longing turned to hurt, knowing it was all about to be yanked away once the door closed and we were back on the road. And who was responsible for that?

"Drive safely, please, Jonnie," she urged. "Happy New Year to you both."

I offered a final nice-to-meet-you, and they stood in the doorway as we walked to Penelope, started the car, and honked and waved while pulling away. I loved that they waited until we were out of sight before they closed the door.

"Don't say it," he said.

I grinned mischievously. *Jonnie.* "I won't. *Right now,*" I said after a beat. He blushed for a second time. "She's the only one who calls you that, huh."

"And I'd like to keep it that way."

"Just remember that the next time you call me Squeaky. I have ammunition now."

It was an empty threat, at best. I had once admitted during a late-night text last fall that I loved my nickname—rather, I loved that it was a term of endearment that came only from him.

"Well, I might as well give you the rest of the hometown tour," said Jon.

"Might as well."

Our blasé delivery betrayed our intentions, yet neither of us copped to it.

Penelope maneuvered through side streets, and Jon pointed out landmarks of a distant past: the mailbox he and his buddies egged one Halloween because the neighborhood curmudgeon refused to give "those rotten kids" any candy; the house where he'd consumed his first beer (and the bushes he'd thrown up in following his second, third, and fourth); the Dunkin' Donuts that had once been a 7-Eleven where he used to buy Pop Rocks and baseball cards. They reminded me of the house Gaia and I believed was haunted, where we dared each other to ring the doorbell on Halloween; the deli where we bought giant shortbread cookies with rainbow sprinkles and ate them before our mom got home; the numerous backyards that became our battlefields for Capture the Flag. We lived parallel suburban lives, Jon and me. Born exactly one month apart, we grew up watching Captain Kangaroo, living in fear of nuclear war, worshipping at the altar of MTV when it actually aired music videos, walking through airports without having to remove one's shoes, and living to regret parachute pants. We'd speculated whether our social orbits would have collided had we lived in the same town and gone to school together. He was on the basketball team and the yearbook and newspaper staffs, while I was on the tennis team and in the jazz ensemble and edited the literary art magazine. We couldn't break-dance. We loved Billy Idol and hated Billy Ocean. We were neither popular nor shunned. We received our fair amount of bullying for preferring books to beer.

Would we have been friends?

Why would we not have? No, the question was, would we have been *more*?

Jon pulled into the parking lot of the high school he'd fictionally named Red Rock Senior High but was in actuality named after some senator, and scenes from *Bleacher Seats* instantly came into focus: to the left, the football field with rusted-out bleachers that had been torn down; to the right, the parking lot used for drag racing that had since been replaced by a new brick science building out of place among the stucco façade of the other building. Clay tennis courts in back. The state, national, and school flags flying in front. I half expected to peer through a dirty window and find the equally fictional Mr. Connors, social studies teacher by day, basketball coach by life; Jennifer Cross, the object of protagonist Elliot Hicks's affection; and the rival badass, Roscoe Bently.

"I know I've said this before, but your flair for description and detail when it comes to place and setting is uncanny," I said. "I feel as if I've already been here."

"Thanks," he said.

"It's something massively lacking in my writing."

"What you lack in setting, you more than compensate for in dialogue," he said.

"Yes, but I've always considered myself to be as much a visual person as I am an aural person. So why can't I do it the way you do it?"

"You're a textbook Jungian extrovert. You don't look at the little picture. Your sense of place comes from *how* you live in it. You make meaning from witness, but that witness is comprised of thinking-feeling-action, not seeing-thinking-processing."

He was spot-on. It was what had made us such good friends in the first place—he got me so well, saw me so clearly, and I him. We seemed to achieve it without even trying. To see evidence of it now, in the aftermath of the heartbreak and the mistakes, was gratifying, not to mention a relief.

"You sure you weren't a psych professor in a former life?" I asked.

"Maybe," he said.

I had been a psychology major in college; although a fat lot of good it did me—I made a living at writing quirky love lives but couldn't figure out my own.

"Hey, we just talked shop. We can officially write off the trip as a business expense now," I said with a grin.

"And we haven't officially gotten on the road yet."

We exchanged glances, and that this-is-really-happening moment hit me again. Real live honest-to-God face time. A face whose prickly stubble I could touch. Eyes with color and definition I could never quite detect in pixels. Blue-gray, I now realized, although practically turquoise in different lighting. With soft, straight lashes and eyebrows the color of roasted almonds. The rest of his hair was almost a caramel hue in direct sunlight, and I could finally see the gray hairs in his sideburns and lining the nape of his neck. His hair was coarse and cowlicked.

And yet, for all his easygoing self-deprecation, I knew that when he joked about envying my obsessive, time-sucking, high-maintenance hair routine that probably would have made even Vidal Sassoon exasperated with me, he was likely telling the truth. Plus, he knew my tastes in men. He'd read my second novel, *Be like Bender*, about a kid who comes of age during the eighties, and knew about my own adolescent crushes on British New Romantics whose mousse consumption matched their musicianship. Alpha males never did it for me. Neither did uniforms. Put a guy in an Armani suit, however, and *hello*. I liked clean-shaven, tapered, layered, well groomed without being too metrosexual. But I also liked a geekish element. Tall, but not gangly. Glasses, but not yuppie.

Jonathan Moss was neither an alpha male nor a metrosexual. He was a guy, that's all. He liked dogs and sports and books and the Moody Blues and Mary Tyler Moore and preferred downtown to the suburbs and had lived and worked just about everywhere, from corporate highrises to family farmhouses.

And me? I was a hybrid in every way. I believed in prayer as much as I believed in scholarly research; I liked Bach as much as I liked the B-52s; I loved lipstick but hated dresses; I preferred Judy Blume to H. P. Lovecraft, cats to dogs, chocolate to vanilla, fruits to vegetables, suburbs to the city, condos to the country. My glass was more than half-full; it runneth over. I was the type of person who would've said, "On the bright side, the play was good," the night Lincoln was shot. I excelled at playing devil's advocate. Jon wasn't a pessimist, more like a pragmatist.

I was flighty. He was grounded. I needed the ocean. He needed the mountains. I needed my own bathroom. He needed his own garage. I needed my family. He needed his work.

Why me, Merriweather? Jon had texted one late night in October, more than a year ago, after he and Shannon had split up, when we knew the seismic shift from platonic to romantic had taken place, neither of us copping to it until that moment.

It was a question I had asked as well: *How could you possibly want this guy*—this *guy, who lives on the other side of the country, who, up until a few months ago, was* married, *who likes the new Muppets rather than the old Muppets? I mean, that's just* wrong.

Because you get me, I'd texted back. And no one had ever gotten me before.

And you're attractive, I now thought. Why had I never told him? Why wouldn't I admit it to him now?

"I'm glad we got to do this," I said. "It's nice to know you this way now. They're not just stories anymore."

"Feels like you can finally see all of me," he said.

You're the only one I've ever wanted to see all of me.

The exposure suddenly felt monstrous. Frightening. Yet another sign that I was in trouble.

"Does it still feel like home, or is it just a place now?"

"A little of both," he said. "It'll always be home. But it's a home from another lifetime. I don't think that's a bad thing. Although it's gotten so that I don't know which is more real—the places I create in my novels or the places I've actually been."

"Both," I said. After giving us time to reflect, I spoke again. "My hometown wasn't much different. Suburban. Middle class. Maybe a little more cosmetic and a lot less arid. And yet Arizona and New York really are about as opposite as it gets."

"I hope to see it sometime."

I folded my arms across my chest. I didn't want him to see my home. If he saw my home, then he'd see my heart. Moreover, I didn't want him to know that last year's late-night what-if was knocking at my door again.

"We should get going," I said. "A lot of miles to cover."

He put the SUV in gear, pulled out of the parking lot, and we left Jonathan Moss's past behind.

Chapter Nine

The road trip "officially" began when we entered the interstate a little after ten o'clock. The moment we merged and the cruise control was set, I closed my eyes and let the rhythm of the road grooves lull me into a semislumber. Jon took advantage of my lack of resistance to punch up his first playlist: an eclectic juxtaposition of country, the Clash, and classic rock.

When I opened my eyes, he was tapping the steering wheel in time to the music with his left hand. A memory of my father clacking his wedding band against the steering wheel met me at that moment. The sound used to be akin to the soothing effect of a boat rocking or the subtle ticktock of a grandfather clock. I used to match him on the rhythm by leaning forward and tapping on the back of the front seat until he ordered me to sit back and buckle my seat belt. I'd wanted to be a drummer before I took piano lessons. I suddenly wondered if I'd switched because of the negative reinforcement. Or was it because I missed my dad setting the beat?

I noticed that Jon's left ring finger still showed a faint tan line where a wedding band had occupied it for nearly ten years, a ghostly shadow. I wondered if maybe the percussive habit was so ingrained that Jon didn't even notice the lack of timbre from the absent ring. The muffled mutation of the sound sans ring was symbolic on several levels—the absence of the wedding band connoting the absence of my father, the abandonment of marriage, my love of drumming . . .

"Are you used to it?" I asked.

"Used to what?"

"Not being married anymore."

He spied his ring finger, as if noticing its nakedness for the first time. "I guess so. It's been almost a year and a half since Shannon and I split up. Ten months since the divorce was final. And it was over before it was over, know what I mean?"

I nodded. "Yeah."

"It doesn't upset me anymore, if that's what you're asking," he said.

"I'm glad."

A few miles of silence passed before he spoke again. "You know, I never thanked you for jumping into that hole with me. A lot of people were supportive, but you were the only one in the trench. And I left you there. I'll always regret that."

I didn't realize until that moment how badly I'd needed to hear both his gratitude and his remorse.

"I guess the important thing is that we both got out. And we're in this car together right now, so something good must have come of it," I said.

"We learned something," he said.

"Indeed."

What had *I* learned? For one thing, *when your male best friend is getting a divorce, for chrissakes don't jump in the hole.* Other than that, I learned that heartbreak is heartbreak even when the romance ends before it begins.

I'd also learned that losing Jonathan as a friend had hurt way more than losing him as a potential lover. It was the routine I'd missed most: the late-morning Messenger chats, the afternoon random where-are-you-now photo exchanges, ranging from Jon's recliner to my walk at the beach to Jon's local greasy spoon to my local bagel place; the good-night text. Smack in the middle of all that breathed a plethora of jokes and stories and confessions and mutual appreciation and compliments and verbal affection.

That doesn't sound like best-friend behavior to me, Hazel had said during one of our lunches following the fallout with Jonathan.

What do you mean?

You and I haven't done half that shit.

I'd looked at her bewildered. *It's not like we were sexting each other or anything like that. We were just having fun. We weren't being intimate. I would never do that with a married man. I never once thought of him as anything more than a friend. Neither did he with me.*

I'm not saying either of you had ulterior motives. I'm just saying you were both clueless. Intimacy is more than cuddling and whatnot.

If that was true, then why hadn't I had that kind of intimacy when a guy was physically in the room? I couldn't think of any beau with whom I'd shared so much of myself in such a casual way, without the threat of loss.

Was that why none of those relationships had ever worked out?

Why had I let myself fall for someone who lived across the country despite my whimsical, romantic—hell, naïve—notion that love had a way of erasing the miles between two people?

Was that the way of all writers? Were we just word people? Or maybe just weirdos. Given a choice between spending four hours in a library and four hours at a celebrity-attended party, I'd choose the library. So would Jonathan. And Hazel. And Kalvin. And ninety percent of the authors I knew.

Then again, it depended on which celebrities were at the party, I suppose. And if they brought books with them.

Thing is, we did eventually sext and flirt and propose to raise the stakes—after his marriage ended. Maybe if we had used those exact words—*raise the stakes*—we wouldn't have done so. But what if we had gone through with the trip last year? Hadn't I been naïve to think a love relationship would materialize as easily as our friendship did in our texts and e-mails and Facebook comments and FaceTime? Would it have fallen apart anyway? Would we have achieved the same level of intimacy in physical proximity had we been consciously attempting to do so? And now, I wondered: What had devastated me more—that the *idea* of the romance had never come to be, or that the romance itself never came to be? Jon was the one who backed out of the road trip last year, so I'd always fixated my hurt on his leaving. Too much like my father. If this was the second chance, then what course of action was I supposed to take here and now?

I left my thoughts and resumed the conversation. "What did *you* learn?" I asked.

"I learned how much of myself I held back in relationships because I was afraid no one would love the real me. I learned my true worthiness."

"What is your true worthiness?"

"Giving and receiving love."

"That sounds more like purpose than worthiness."

"Maybe. But how could I achieve it if I didn't believe myself worthy of it?"

He'd expressed the desire, practically craved it, shortly after his marriage ended in the spring: *I just want to give and receive love. Why is that so hard?* And my response, the one I'd not shared, was *Well, geez, Jon. I can be the one for you to give love to and receive it from.* Because that was the precise moment when I'd stopped thinking about Jon as a friend and started feeling something way deeper. And it had terrified me because it meant I could lose him. And I did. Perhaps I had somehow given in to the self-fulfilling prophecy by playing into the fear.

Friendship could be enough. It had to be.

"So listen, anytime you want a food or bathroom or stretch-your-legs break, let me know," he said. "We have a destination in that I made a hotel reservation, but it won't kill anyone to be an hour off or whatever."

He said: *I made a hotel reservation.*

I heard: *We're going to spend the night in a hotel room for the first time ever.*

Sure, I established the separate-beds rule, but still. He was going to see me in pajamas and with bed head in the morning. He was going to hear me snore and possibly see me drool. He could even somehow get a whiff of my morning breath. He was going to have to deal with me pre-coffee. If we were just friends, then I shouldn't care about that, right?

"OK," I said.

Understatement of the Year.

"You still OK with sharing the room?"

"I don't know," I said. "At least, I won't know until we're there. It sounded fine in theory, but to think of it now . . ."

"Say the word and I'll get separate rooms. My dime."

"Jon, no. I should pay my way. I have an objective here—to attend my father's memorial."

From my peripheral vision, I saw him frown.

"It's just odd," I added. "A grown man and woman sharing a double room." I tried to gauge his reaction but failed. My mind-reading skills weren't good. "But since it's completely platonic . . ."

Jon snickered. I had no trouble reading that one. And it irked me. Did he really think I was being sarcastic? Or worse, disingenuous?

"What," I said.

He shook his hand dismissively. "It's all good, Sage," he said. I decided not to press him.

My seat remained in a slightly reclined position, so I leaned back and watched the scenery move past me like a filmstrip, frame by frame, in rapid motion. In contrast to the Northeast, trees were nonexistent along this part of the interstate. The horizon line was set far off into the distance, the sun straight out of a sci-fi doomsday movie in that it hovered directly above us, ready to scorch everything within reach, even though the temperature had yet to hit seventy degrees. I watched the broken lines of the lane dividers pass like a conveyor belt, flattened, as if they were moving and the car was still. Jon queued up a second playlist: the Best of Steely Dan. He kept his eyes fixed on the road and tapped the steering wheel in rhythm. I stared out the side and counted cars with state license plates other than Arizona, wondering what the hell I was doing in this car.

CHAPTER TEN

Other than Jon insisting on singing along with the entire Steely Dan catalog as he drove, neither of us spoke much until a sign appeared informing us that we were within a hundred miles of the Grand Canyon. I pointed to it. "Too bad we can't go," I said.

He unsuccessfully quashed a smile.

"Wait—are we?" I said.

"You've never seen it, so . . . yeah. I wanted it to be a surprise."

My mood pulled a one-eighty. "It is?! This is so cool!" Jon all-out smiled now.

The traffic slowed as if on cue.

"Hmm," said Jon. "Unusual for this stretch of road."

"Maybe there's construction," I said.

"Or an accident."

"Or maybe it's just holiday traffic? People still have parties to go to."

"Not around here. This isn't the Northeast," he said, and quickly apologized for what sounded like a criticism. Moments later, he silenced the music. "So if you could invite anyone in the world to dinner, who would it be?"

"Excuse me?" I asked.

"Just asking," he said sheepishly. "So . . . fantasy dinner guest?"

"Alan Alda," I replied.

He gave me a cryptic look. "How come?"

"He was the first person that popped into my head."

"Why?"

"Why not?" I said. "Did I ever tell you about the time my mom ran into him at the supermarket? Like, literally. With her shopping cart. Accidentally, of course."

"Awesome. You know the *M*A*S*H* episodes he wrote never held up as well as the ones Larry Gelbart wrote."

I concurred. "It all went downhill after McLean Stevenson and Wayne Rogers left. Although there were a couple of really good episodes, like the interview in black and white, and the one with the guy who thinks he's Jesus Christ."

"I fucking loved those," said Jon.

"Best sitcom from the seventies?" I asked.

"*All in the Family*," he replied. "No contest."

"Agreed. But I thought you would've said *The Mary Tyler Moore Show*."

"A very close second. By a hair."

"OK, so what about your dinner guest?"

He contemplated his response. "I'm trying to decide whether to go with the lofty answer or the superficial one."

"What's the first name that came to mind?" I asked.

"My grandpa Charles," he said, the name weighted in wistfulness. "He died when I was ten. Way too soon for us to appreciate each other as human beings, to learn from one another, to have a meaningful conversation."

"My maternal grandmother died when I was twenty. She was pretty fantastic," I said. "After my dad left, we didn't really keep in touch with his side of the family."

"So you lost more than your dad," said Jon.

He said it so matter-of-factly, but the truth of it fell on me like a tree trunk. Strange how I had forgotten that. Forgotten about how my aunt Janice used to pinch my cheeks and give me five-dollar bills for my birthday, and my aunt Anne took Gaia and me to the Bronx Zoo. Forgotten my cousins Tommy and Mark and Edward and Marybeth. I didn't even keep up with them on Facebook. Tears came to my eyes.

"I guess I did," I said quietly.

Jon was silent for a moment, as if thinking about whether he should address it. I didn't want him to. Maybe he was sorry for having said anything.

"Grandpa Charles would have liked your spunkiness," he said.

I perked up. "I'm spunky?"

"You went through with this trip, didn't you? That takes spunk."

"Or stupidity."

"Well, yeah," he said with a wink. "Anyway, I would love to see my grandpa again. But the question specifies 'in the world,' so I should probably name someone living. I'd have to go with Paul McCartney."

"You memorized your own question?"

The sheepish look was back. "It's a reporter thing, I guess. OK, next question."

"You've got a list?"

He ignored me. "Would you like to be famous?"

"Jon, we've discussed that, like, how many times?"

The answer, for both of us, was *no*. We enjoyed having loyal readers (we rarely used the word *fans*, although we had those as well), and we loved that we had sold enough books to make a living as authors. But we each had yet to be recognized in a public place, and we were both fine with that.

"Right," he said. "OK, soooo . . ." He trailed off.

"I would love to be a *Jeopardy* clue," I said.

Jon concurred. "Oh yeah, that would be the shit. Next question."

I eyed him suspiciously. "What's with the icebreaker interrogation?" I asked.

"I'm just making conversation."

"We've never had trouble making conversation before. And these don't sound like Jonathan Moss questions. These sound like canned questions you downloaded from some blog post on developing social skills for parties."

Jon became cross. "Thanks a lot, Sage. That really makes a person feel good."

"I'm just saying—"

"Forget it," he said, and turned the music on again. *Shit.*

The SUV suddenly felt about the size of my Beetle.

We drove in silence for about fifteen minutes. Fifteen minutes of that sticky, gooey silence—even despite the Led Zeppelin blaring—that makes you want to jump out of your skin if someone doesn't say something soon. I didn't know if we'd just entered a game of chicken or if neither of us genuinely had anything to say. All I could think about in those fifteen minutes was how maybe Gaia had been right and I'd made a huge mistake agreeing to this trip.

Seriously though—who would I want as a dinner guest? Where did he come up with that?

And yet the more I thought about it, the more it struck me that I had heard those questions once before. Or maybe I'd asked my hair clients those types of questions in my former career.

I had to admit that I had been rude, however. Jon had a right to feel stung.

"I'm sorry for what I said," I started. My voice practically echoed in the car. "It was mean and unwarranted."

Jon kept his eyes on the road. "It's OK," he finally said.

"We can continue with the questions," I offered.

"Forget it," he replied. "You're right. They were stupid."

"I never said they were stupid, Jon."

"I just thought that since we've got so many miles to cover and hours to kill . . ."

"So let's do it. It will be fun."

Jon half smiled. "There's a list in the glove box."

"So you *did* download and memorize them!" I said in an *Aha!* kind of tone.

"Guilty," he said.

"Well, let's see them," I said, as I opened the glove box and pulled out the paper, tri-folded and double-sided. I unfurled it and skimmed the first few questions, hoping carsickness wouldn't hit me.

"Wait a minute—I know these," I said.

And then it hit me: earlier in the year, a *New York Times* article had gone viral in which the writer personally (and successfully) applied the theory that two people could fall in love in a controlled environment. Researchers partnered strangers, male and female, gave them a set of questions (the ones I was currently holding in my hands), and instructed the participants to engage in a dialogue answering each question, sitting at a table opposite each other. The kicker, however, according to the article, was that afterward they had to stare into each other's eyes for four minutes. Turned out the writer and her "subject" had fallen in love.

At the time, the article's going viral had coincided with my hiding Jon on Facebook and cutting all communication with him. I'd read it against my better judgment, meaning I'd read it knowing I'd leave it either desperately wishing I could meet and fall in love with someone *that* way—it was so much less complicated than the alternatives, especially the one that had just blown up in my face—or feeling the crushing regret of never having had the opportunity to look Jonathan Moss in the eye in person, be it for four minutes or four seconds. Worse still, the likelihood that we ever would had been snuffed out. No, the only time we'd come face-to-face was if Mammoth Publishing was going to shell out for another New York shindig and bring all their authors under one roof again. Given how many new authors they'd signed in the last two years, they'd have to rent Grand Central Station.

As it turned out, I wound up with both the envy and the regret. Total suckitude.

From a fan-fiction perspective, I would have loved to play out the experiment with any character I'd ever had a crush on, like John Bender from *The Breakfast Club*, and place myself in their world to see if they could succumb to the same circumstances. Perhaps the entire experiment could take place in an elevator. Or back at that high school library in Shermer, Illinois. Or I fantasized about confronting some guy I'd had a one-sided crush on, getting him in a room, and doing the experiment. In turn, he would become unblinded by whatever had made him overlook me as a potential lover. Whether I still wanted him would then be up to me.

Which then made me realize that perhaps Jon had gotten a similar idea, and not for a novel.

"You *asshole*," I snarled.

"Hang on, Sage," he started, but I was too livid to listen.

"Do you have any idea how much reading this article wrecked me? No, of course you don't. You couldn't. And yet, here you are, using it as some ploy."

"It's not a ploy."

Like hell it wasn't. "Ugh, I did it again. I trusted that your intentions were genuine."

"My intentions *were* genuine," he said. "Look, I can't stop wondering whether we really did avoid disaster or made the biggest mistake of our lives by not taking this trip a year ago. And not just the trip—by not taking a chance on *us*. I just wanted to find out once and for all."

"Why now?"

Elisa Lorello

"Haven't you ever come to a point in your life when you can't *not* do it? When you stop and look at your life and all you can think is: *not this*. I had that moment in my marriage, but I was too afraid to end it because I didn't know what came after it. I let fear of the unknown rule over my misery. I didn't want to do that again. Life was just fine, except it was missing you. *I* was missing you. And I finally realized: *not this*. I don't want a just fine life if you're not a part of it. And even though I had no idea what the outcome would be, I couldn't not take a chance."

I've had *not this* moments. When I sat in the break room between clients writing stories rather than gossiping with the other stylists. When one day, in the middle of doing foil highlights, I stepped outside of myself and saw someone who no longer belonged there. I'd made a plan that day:

1. Reduce as much debt as possible.
2. Write for one hour every night after work, and two hours on Saturday and Sunday.
3. Be published within two years.

The scariest and most exciting day had been when I quit my job after signing my publishing contract—almost two years to the date of my plan—and received my first royalty advance. The advance quickly dissolved in monthly expenses, however, and the book took almost one year to earn out. At one point I thought I might have to move back in with my mom. But the thought of going back to the salon day after day, on my feet, listening to other people's stories rather than telling my own, was enough of a motivator. I'd make a living as a writer one way or another. So I wrote articles for *Modern Salon* and other cosmetology industry magazines until my second novel launched and catapulted up the Amazon Best Seller list.

The leap had been invigorating as much as it had been terrifying. I'd never felt so free. But it struck me that maybe my father had experienced the same thing with us. What was it about our family that made him say, *not this*? What had my mother done or not done, said or not said? What about our house or home life was unappealing? Why weren't Gaia and I *this* rather than *not this*? Had he ever been fearful about the prospect of life without Mom and Gaia and me? Was he excited? Did he ever have a regret? Or did he think he'd waited too long?

These were the questions I wished I'd asked him while he was still alive, and I could only hope to get some answers when I went to Sacramento the day after tomorrow.

To know Jon had a *not this* regarding me left me breathless. I wondered if I would have come to that same moment about him. Or was that why I'd ultimately decided to go on this road trip—because I couldn't *not* do it?

"Why not start over the way we did the first time around, with texts and e-mails and whatnot?" I asked. "Why the road trip?"

"Do you know of any better way to make the leap?"

"Are you on crack? Did you hit your head and lose your memory? When *you* decided *you* wanted us to just be friends, *you* were the one who touted, 'Romance can't be contrived.' *You* were the one who said, 'I wanted to want it, but you just can't force these things.' *You* were the one who said, 'I lied to myself when I said I was OK with this long-distance thing.' Now you want to play this little game?"

"It's not a game."

I'd never actually seen or heard him unnerved before. I'd seen it in typeface, but never heard the inflection and the change in pitch of his vocal cords. I'd never seen the furrow of his brow or the color of his cheeks or the tightness of his lips. It incited the same uneasy feeling in me as the words on the screen had done.

"Oh, right. It's an experiment. We're caged in this car like lab rats, in a controlled environment. Except the last thing we are is random strangers—I mean, sure, we've barely spoken to each other for the better part of the year, but we're way past the getting-to-know-you stage, don't you think?"

"No, I don't. We already built a foundation of friendship. Let's add some bricks now. Too many times the relationship starts with plenty of bricks and no foundation. That's why I wanted us to ask and answer these questions. I wanted to see what we'd build."

I didn't want to build anything. I wanted to jump out of the SUV while it was still moving.

"No, Jon," I said. "This isn't what I signed up for. I signed up for a road trip so we could reconnect as friends and have some fun."

"And go to your father's memorial," he interjected.

I grimaced. "And go to my father's memorial, yes. But that's all. We're not going to try to be anything more."

Since when?

"You weren't afraid a year ago," he said.

"I was stupid a year ago."

"But you are afraid now," he said. "Of what?"

"For starters, what happens once this 'experiment' is over. Did you consider the consequences? How do we go about our merry way if one of us"—a.k.a. *me*—"winds up more 'invested' than the other? What if it all blows up in our faces again? What if you walk out yet again? Fool me once, shame on you . . ." I started.

Jonathan looked close to blowing a gasket. "I've got my shit together. You've got your shit together. We've had time and space to heal. I got counseling and my divorce came through and I'm trying to correct the dumbass things I said and did when I didn't have my shit together."

"You should have left well enough alone," I said.

"And you shouldn't have agreed to this trip," he countered.

The seat belt across my chest suddenly enclosed me like a strait-jacket as my stomach turned over with dread. The SUV had become downright claustrophobic. We were shackled inside, an invisible smog of tension suffocating us, while the traffic inched. Worse still, we had another ninety miles before we reached the Grand Canyon. Not to mention the rest of today and an additional three days of driving.

"We're not going anywhere," I said after a prolonged stretch of silence and watching each car crawl ahead with the same restraint and frustration.

"I'll say," he muttered under his breath. I narrowed my eyes at him in a fiery glower, long enough so he could feel its heat.

I searched past the line of immobile cars for police or ambulance lights, roadwork signs, or any clue to let us in on the secret.

"This blows," I said.

"Want to get out and walk? Because I'd be happy to let you out here."

This time I faced him, making sure he could see me directly, and I shot him a death glare. "Go to hell, Jon."

We had exchanged angry words before, but never had we put a physical voice or inflection to them. And never had I gone that far.

"Right back at you," he retorted.

"All you had to do was be honest with me from the very beginning," I said.

"I *was* honest with you from the very beginning. I told you I loved you. I also told you my heart had been shattered. I told you I didn't know what was going to happen. I told you I didn't want to hurt you."

"No, you went from *I love you* to *I'm not there yet*. You went from *How soon is now* to *No no no no no*. You yo-yoed me with *come here, come here, come here*, then *get away, get away, get away*. You're the one who suggested we go out for dinner and a movie for the rest of our lives, and then freaked out when I said *OK*."

"You've made it clear on several occasions that I'm the one who fucked everything up," said Jon, "but don't play the innocent victim here. Where was *your* judgment, knowing how much I was struggling back then, how confused and depressed I was, how erratic my behavior was? Alarms went off like bullhorns, and you headed straight for the iceberg anyway."

"So, this was all *my* fault?"

"You know I'm not saying that. I'm saying it takes two to get it this wrong. And I've apologized enough. Either forgive me or get the fuck out of this car."

Oh, the things I wanted to do at that moment—smack him across his face, throw cold coffee at him, sock him in his vulnerable groin. Tweet *Jonathan Moss is an insufferable douche bag.* That last one would surely backfire, given that he would retweet it the moment he saw it, and all his loyal readers would pile on me.

As I sat and fumed, I couldn't deny that Jon was right about one thing: behind all that anger was *fear.* Fear of what could happen were I to actually go through with this experiment. Things could go horribly wrong all over again.

Or things could go horribly *right.*

And wasn't that the scarier of the two?

What if Jonathan Moss and I fell in love for real this time, face-to-face? What if we became truly intimate with each other in all those ways you can't behind the screen of a smartphone?

Hadn't we already started? Does it get more intimate than parking on a cozy love seat, perusing family photos, and sharing memories? Wasn't *this* intimate—the two of us in a car, driving across country, nothing between us and the road?

What if the second chance wasn't about being friends or falling in love? What if it was about the other side of it—the prospect of *not* falling in love, *not* being together, *not* working it out—and being OK regardless?

What if the second chance was choosing a different response to *not this*?

I wasn't ready to face that yet.

Thirty minutes later, after scraping over no more than a mile on the interstate, Jon veered off the first exit he could, drove for another hour blasting a playlist of Chuck Berry, Buddy Holly, and, inexplicably, Radiohead, in an attempt to drown out our stony silence before finally pulling off the main road and into a town with a gas station and food court. We stretched our legs and arms and used the restrooms, and he bought a chicken sandwich and a Coke from a sub shop while I stood on line at a kiosk to order a stuffed pita. Despite the chilly morning, the temperature had surpassed the predictions and climbed to seventy-five degrees at noon, so we found a clean, empty table outdoors and ate without speaking and used the restrooms a second time and met back at Penelope. Jon pulled her up to the gas pumps, topped off the tank, and squeegeed the windshield.

He reentered the SUV and turned to me.

"Here's the deal. Yes, I wanted us to start over as friends and see where it would go from there. Yes, I wanted us to have a second chance at a trip that always had the potential to be fabulous. Yes, I know I gave you every reason to question my sincerity when I let you down last year and sent you more mixed signals than a third-base coach. But I beg of you, Sage, let's talk civilly to each other. We always promised we'd be kind to one another. We've not been kind today. I don't mind disagreements. I don't even mind arguing. But please. Argue kindly. My heart has endured way too much unnecessary roughness."

I failed to hold back the tears that had forced their way out.

"I'm sorry for telling you to go to hell," I said, wiping my cheeks with a paper napkin from the stack I'd pilfered from the kiosk.

"Me too," he said. "I really am."

"And for calling you an asshole."

"And for telling you to get the fuck out of this car."

He leaned over and pulled me to him in a sideways embrace, and I breathed in the fabric softener scent along with fast food and gasoline. His touch was charged yet also grounding, and it simultaneously made me want to draw closer and pull farther away. Why didn't any other man's touch ever make me feel this way? Of course my exes had turned me on. They'd been loving and passionate and sexy. But none ever made me feel . . . *alive.*

Jon let go and we returned to our sides. *We should hug more often.*

With nothing more to say, he turned the ignition, put the car in gear, and, not wanting to return to the creeping crawl on the interstate, consulted the GPS app for a different route.

Our silence was now the result of trying to figure out what path our conversation should take as well—side streets of small talk or a new, less familiar road of starting over? I don't think either of us knew where we were headed, in both cases.

I reached for the paper and perused it again.

"Well, we covered the first two," I said. "Number three asks whether you rehearse what you're going to say before you call someone."

Jon looked at me, perplexed. And then he smiled softly, serenely, one of acceptance and allowance and pleasure yet devoid of expectation. "We're fucking writers," he said with a snicker. "How could we *not* rehearse?"

I laughed and said, "No shit," followed by, "Hey, I have an idea. Instead of answering these questions ourselves, let's try to guess what the other person would answer."

"That goes against the rules of the experiment."

"Well, given that we're not random strangers, I'd say we've already broken protocol, which makes the experiment moot."

"I guess. Well then, let's just have fun and see how well we really know each other," he said amiably. "But we should still do the looking-in-each-other's-eyes-for-four-minutes thing when we're done."

"Why?" I asked.

"Why not?" he said, echoing my earlier reply.

"I don't think we'll last ten seconds. We'll be too busy giggling like Beavis and Butt-Head."

He paused for yet another beat. "You're probably right."

"Let's just do this instead," I suggested.

"Sure thing."

His compliance should have appeased me. But suddenly I felt cheated, even though I was the one who'd encouraged it.

Chapter Eleven

We reached the Grand Canyon approximately ninety minutes and eight questions later, stopping at number eleven. In response to number five, I correctly guessed that the last time Jon had sung to himself was in the car on the way to Phoenix, and that he sang Christmas carols with his family a week ago (we decided that constituted singing to someone else). And although he didn't know to whom I'd sung, he correctly guessed the song was "Happy Birthday," and the last time I'd sung to myself was in the shower.

For number four, which asked us to describe a perfect day, we turned to the silly:

Jon's day, as dictated by Sage—

7:00 a.m.: Breakfast of pancakes, bacon, maple syrup, coffee, a little more bacon, and a strawberry just for a hint of color.

"What about my workout?" he asked. "I'll need it after that freak breakfast."

"This is Fantasyland," I replied. "Who works out in Fantasyland?"

9:00 a.m.: Write two chapters of mega-bestselling novel, because Jon has figured out the secret formula to writing the mega-bestselling novel, and he's not telling anyone! Hint: it contains bats and fornication.

11:00 a.m.: Nap.

12:00 p.m.: Turn self into a fly, go wherever self wants, and actually be a fly on the wall.

1:00 p.m.: Lunch at Waffle House.

2:00 p.m.: Beam self to Manhattan and do something touristy, like go to the top of the Empire State Building. Attempt to drop a water balloon from the observation deck. (Although in real life you'd likely be arrested for terrorism if you even were spotted with said water balloon.)

Jon countered: "Actually, I'd love to visit the Statue of Liberty someday. For real."

"You should," I said.

"*We* should," he countered.

And wow, did *that* give me all the feels. We used to say things like "We should hang out"—at a coffee shop, the Rock and Roll Hall of Fame, a public library—in the vein of companionship. But the way he just said *we* . . . it was so beyond casual companionship. Much like the proposed road trip had become one year ago. And just like I had done then, I allowed myself to contemplate what *we* would look like in iconic, romantic New York places like Rockefeller Center and the

Prometheus statue, or the Plaza Hotel or Strawberry Fields in Central Park. Well, they were romantic to me, at least.

> 4:00 p.m.: Sex.

He raised his eyebrows. "With whom?" he asked.

"Julianne Moore, of course," I replied.

He smiled bashfully, seemingly appreciative that I remembered his celebrity crush.

"You certainly have my best interests at heart."

"Well, come on—what perfect day wouldn't include sex?"

"And you think you're not spunky, Merriweather," he said, shaking his head with mock incredulity.

I'd just broken Rule Number One. Like, big-time. I hadn't even realized it until I felt the jolt of current from the exchange. Why had I even gone there in the first place?

Because it felt easy, that's why. Scintillating. Fun.

"Sorry," I said.

"For what?"

"For the sex talk."

He laughed. "We're grown-ups."

"I'm just saying, we're breaking the rules."

"Ah, yes. The rules."

"We need to take the rules seriously."

He backpedaled. "You're right, Sage. I'm sorry for making light of them."

> 5:00 p.m.: Jam session with five of the world's best guitarists. Blow them away with mastery of "Smoke on the Water." (You have to be a guitarist to get the joke.)

"Sex for an hour? That's pretty good for a fortysomething guy."

"Jon!" I scolded. "The rules. I mean it. Stop."
He apologized again.

7:00 p.m.: Watch sunset.

9:00 p.m.: Eat a meal cooked by an Italian grandmother.
In Italy.

11:00 p.m.: Bed. Partner optional.

"Hang on—who's violating the rules now?" asked Jon.

"I didn't mention anyone specific. Or doing anything with said partner other than sleeping."

"Those are some mighty fine hairs you're splitting, Squeaky. A bed partner can conjure quite the sensual image—spooning, naked, limbs intertwined, lips to the shoulder, hair tangled—"

I cut him off. "OK, I got it. Forget it, no bed partner." I said, in need of a blast of cold air.

SAGE'S DAY, AS TOLD BY JON—

10:00 a.m.: ("I know you like to sleep late," he said.) Wake
up to perfect hair and take shower, in which mega-bestselling
novel idea is born. Hint: Also contains bats and fornication,
except the bats get makeovers first.

"Does my perfect hair get ruined in the shower?" I asked. "Because I don't want to have to redo my hair if it's already perfect. Which means I'd need a shower cap. Which means my hair would be less than perfect coming out of the shower. I don't want to have to do all this work on a perfect day."

Jon laughed. "Well, shit. OK, let's just say you take a shower and your hair miraculously comes out perfect without having to do anything."

11:00 a.m.: French toast for breakfast. Made on French bread. Possibly by a Frenchman. Speaking French.

12:00 p.m: Go to a beach on Long Island and read a book.

"Although you might change your mind if you saw the Pacific," said Jon.

2:00 p.m.: Write the world's greatest love story.

OK, now the sirens went off. Sirens and bells and banging drums. Forget the romantic implications of what he just suggested. The words were damn sparks. The match struck against the stone. Two twigs rubbed together. In terms of genre, I wasn't a romance novelist, but each and every one of my novels had been love stories in one form or another. And no doubt I had been either compensating for a love life that had never quite measured up to reality or persistently searching for the key to manifesting the dream. And what was the dream? What had I longed for my entire life? Not Prince Charming. Not perfection. Just . . . *home*.

3:00 p.m.: Live the world's greatest love story.

My God. Little heart attacks in my chest.

I wanted it. Badly. I'd wanted it all my life. Since my father left and every dream no longer seemed attainable. At least not in the relationship realm. Being a novelist was never a dream as much as an ambition fulfilled. Maybe that was my mistake—classifying love as a dream that had to "come true" rather than be fulfilled.

What if we were doing both right this moment? What if every answered question, each one its own narrative, was narrating the bigger story—the story of us: Merriweather and Moss (Moss and Merriweather)? First we write it, then we live it?

5:00 p.m.: Sex with that guy from that British band.

"Again with the sex!" I chided. "RULE NUMBER ONE. Come on, man!"

"Look, you started it! Why should I deprive you when you gave me celebrity sex?"

Damn if it wasn't all so much fun.

I gave in. "Which guy?"

"You know, the guy with the tight pants and the hair and the hat."

"So . . . all of them?" I asked.

10:00 p.m.: Cake.

"No dinner?" I asked.

"Who needs dinner after all that sex and cake?" he asked.

Good point.

Thing is, he probably wasn't too far off from how I would have imagined it.

~

When we arrived at Grand Canyon National Park, we stepped out of the car and stretched.

"Do we have time to hike a little bit?" I asked.

"I don't know about *hiking*, but sure, we can walk around," said Jon.

The temperature was considerably cooler given the altitude. Luckily, Jon knew to take a sweatshirt and gallantly offered it to me when he saw goose bumps the size of actual geese bubbling on my arms. That Jonathan Moss scent—fabric softener (and was that really his natural scent, or did he just use a shit-ton of Downy on his clothes?) mixed with a little bit of sweat this time—completely enveloped me. Protected me in his warmth. And yet I looked like a little kid wearing a grown-up's shirt.

We set out for the observation deck and casually strolled. When we arrived at the lookout point, I was surprised to find it populated even in December during the holiday week.

Magnificent.

Some things couldn't be captured on a camera, especially one that doubled as a pocket-sized computer. I had to commit this one to memory. The panorama was vast and expansive, the rocks like giant clay formations fresh out of the solar kiln, in an orangey red that no Crayola crayon or Redken hair dye would ever be able to replicate. I took in a breath and only managed to roll out a clichéd "Wow."

"I know," said Jon.

"How many times have you been here?"

"Only a few. Twice when I was a kid—once with my family and once on a field trip. And Shannon and I visited it too."

A wave of disappointment hit me. Not that I was jealous because she got to see it with him first—it would have been foolish to think that they didn't come here en route to or from one of their many visits with Jonathan's family. But I suddenly longed for a way to make it our own. And not just with a selfie.

Jonathan led me to the railing. "Get a good look," he said.

So I looked. Down.

The canyon was deep. And high. And *big*.

Too big.

All of it was too big. Big and bottomless and threatening to suck me in and break every bone in my body and smash me.

I began to feel woozy as vertigo took over.

"You OK, Sage?" I heard Jon ask, sounding farther away than right beside me.

"I think I need some water," I said. My legs turned to jelly.

"Can you make it to the car, or do you need me to carry you?"

"Um, I'm not exactly a supermodel," I said. "I doubt you can lift me two inches off the ground, much less carry me. Plus, I don't need—"

With that he scooped me up and proceeded to walk as I clasped my hands around his neck. He didn't even flinch from the weight.

For the first time in my life, I knew more than an embrace. For the first time I knew the feeling of *I've got you and I'm not going to drop you. You're safe.*

"What, do you pull pickup trucks with your teeth too?"

"I worked on a cattle ranch in New Mexico when I was a teenager. And no, I am not comparing you to a cow."

So this was what it was like to be swept off my feet by Jonathan Moss. The thought amused me until I felt the impact of its truth. We hadn't been on this trip for twenty-four hours, and already I was fighting the temperature of his touch, the spark of his smile, the grace of his presence, the power of his words.

I looked at the path behind me, over his shoulder. The view looked different from his eye level. Seeing the world in new ways.

He didn't have far to carry me. When we reached Penelope, Jon carefully set me on my feet and opened the back door while I leaned against the bumper. He pulled a bottle of water from a shrink-wrapped bulk pack in the stowing area, twisted the cap off, and handed it to me.

"Sip, don't chug," he said. "I'm sorry it isn't cold."

"It's OK," I said. "*I'm* OK. The height got to me, that's all. Plus, I'm a little dehydrated." I steadily felt myself normalizing, my feet more solid on the ground, my legs regaining their muscle and bone.

"You sure? Maybe we should cancel the Vegas reservation and just stay here in town tonight."

"I thought we were going to Los Angeles."

"You've never been to Vegas. I thought it would be fun." Before I could retort, he shot back, "And no, I wasn't planning on getting you drunk and then getting us hitched. I have standards, you know. I'd buy you dinner first."

My heart pounded in Pavlovian-esque behavior to the word *hitched*. And what was more unnerving—the fact that we'd both thought the same thing or that he knew it?

"It'd have to be a really good dinner," I countered.

"Well, that's the difference between us, Merriweather. If you caught me at the right moment, I'd probably marry you if you offered me nothing more than a Pop-Tart and a glass of Tang."

His sincerity practically knocked the wind out of me. What was "the right moment"? I wondered. I was about to ask him when he put his hand on my shoulder, as if to steady me.

"Seriously, are you OK?"

No, I'm not OK. My estranged best friend and I are making marriage jokes and I'm liking it. A lot. It has to stop.

"I'm OK, Jon. Let's go to Vegas."

"Fine by me. It's about four hours away. Five if we stop to eat. Tack on another hour for gas fill-ups and bathroom breaks. Doable. But if you change your mind, then say the word and we'll find a town and someplace else to stay for the night."

Jon escorted me to the passenger side, helped me in, and closed the door. Then he rushed to his side to start the SUV and crank up the air-conditioning.

We left the park and hopped on the interstate and didn't say a word. And yet the silence didn't feel awkward. My mind was occupied with other things—touring Jon's neighborhood, sitting on the love seat looking at photos, the Grand Canyon, me in his arms, wearing his sweatshirt, answering questions designed to determine whether intimacy can be contrived, and Jon's everything-but-outright marriage proposal.

A good twenty minutes passed between us.

"It's going well so far, don't you think?" I said.

We both cracked up.

We never did get that selfie.

Chapter Twelve

We arrived in Las Vegas and all its neon glory close to 7:30 p.m. Pacific Time, both of us exhausted. We'd tackled more questions from the list, detouring on tangents and telling stories and correcting each other when we'd guessed the wrong answer for the other person. And although we weren't officially keeping score, more often than not we were getting it right with each other.

Number seven wanted us to reveal any intuition about how we would die.

Me: Natural causes, according to Jon.

"You're going to live to be a hundred and fifty years old," said Jon.

Jon: Heart attack following all-you-can-eat burrito marathon at age eighty-five, according to me.

"One can only hope," said Jon.

For number eight, we agreed on the three things we appeared to have in common: Being writers. Being sports fans. Being fucked up.

We took the easy way out on that one, knowing we had similarities and shared interests that were much more personal—dare I say, intimate—such as our favorite sound being that of snow falling, or how neither of us ever felt comfortable with casual dating.

Number nine asked us what we felt most grateful for.

Our answers for each other were the same: to be able to make a living doing what we love.

For number ten, which was one of those hindsight questions in which you had to change something about the way you were raised, we gave our own answers instead of guessing what the other would say.

Me: To have pursued novel writing at an earlier age and not listened to those who said there was no money in it.

Jon: To have worn better socks.

We'd stopped for dinner two hours ago and were probably the only two people in town who were planning to veg out in the hotel room and watch Netflix from a laptop. We were also probably the only two people who booked a Comfort Inn rather than one of the gaudy, glitzy hotels you always saw advertised on television commercials.

Not to mention we were also probably the only two people not having sex that night.

After we checked in, we hoofed down the hall to our room, lugging our stuff. OK, my stuff mostly.

"Aw, fuck," said Jon upon opening the door and taking the first steps inside the room.

"What?" I said, his body blocking my view of what had provoked the expletive. He stepped out of the way, and then I saw.

One bed.

One bed?

One bed!

A king-size, but still.

"Aw, fuck," I said.

Jon and I stomped back down the hall and to the lobby, where he argued with the desk clerk about having reserved a double room. The clerk looked at us dubiously.

"I'm sorry, sir, but we had a problem with our online reservation system. It booked more rooms than we had available. I'm afraid all we have is the single."

"Well, you've got a problem, don't you," said Jon.

"It's the holidays, sir. Las Vegas is a popular destination at this time of year."

"So is Times Square," I piped in, realizing that I didn't exercise badassness as much as I stated a simple fact, which did nothing to remedy our predicament. I blushed.

"We can send up a cot, if you want," said the clerk.

Jon and I exchanged glances. "Do you want to look for another place to stay?" I asked him.

He shook his head. "Everything's probably booked." He turned back to the desk clerk. "No cot. Just bring us two extra sets of pillows. And we expect our stay to be comped."

The clerk looked at us like we were stuck in a bad *Happy Days* episode—which, let's face it: we were—but he promised to accommodate us.

Well. That was a game changer.

First thought: *I'll need to keep breath mints next to the bed.*

Second thought: *I'll need to wear one of those nose-strip thingies to keep from snoring.*

Third thought: *Those two things, plus the pajamas—which aren't so much pajamas as they are black spandex bicycle shorts and an oversized purple Henley T-shirt—are certain to win me the So Not the Sexiest Woman Alive Award.*

Fourth thought: *Jon and I are going to share a bed, Jon and I are going to share a bed, Jon and I are going to share a bed . . .*

The corresponding emotion to each thought was along the lines of *shit, shit, shit, SHIT!*

I should have insisted we look for another place to stay, one with two beds or two rooms or two hallways where we could sleep as far away from each other as possible. But the tug-of-war was back, with the *hell yeah*s battling the *no way*s. Part of me wanted to push myself, to be curious, to let things unfold as they may. The other part of me wanted to scream, "Plot twist!" and rewind back to me coming down the stairs in the Phoenix airport, first thing out of my mouth being, "We ain't sleeping together, Mossy. Ain't goin' there." Hell, rewind back to the night I officially said yes to this road trip and change my answer to No. Freaking. Way.

Jon and I returned to the room and stood in front of the bed taking in the space, as if flummoxed by it all. And how did *he* feel about this? I wondered. I tried to imagine little people-emotions, like in the movie *Inside Out*, sitting at a console in Jonathan's head. For some reason I pictured them all looking like different-colored Cookie Monsters. Must have been very chaotic in there.

Or maybe it was all cut-and-dried to him.

"It's a big bed, at least," I said.

"I'm a big guy," said Jon.

"Why didn't you accept the cot?"

"Do *you* want to sleep on a cot?" he asked.

"No," I said.

"Neither do I."

"But one of us probably should." I pointed to the love seat against the far wall. "I can curl up on that, if you want."

"No. This is stupid. We're mature adults, not Joanie and Chachi. I think we can sleep in a goddamn bed together and keep our hands and appendages to ourselves. Besides, we're both so freaking tired, we'll be zonked out the minute we turn off the lights."

He said *appendages*. I silently giggled. Yeah. Totally mature.

I took in a breath. *Yes, I can do this. We're friends, after all. Just friends. Nothing more. Never will be anything more. Just keep telling yourself that.*

My legs weren't shaved. Dammit.

"I should tell you that I snore," I said.

"Me too," he replied.

"That's OK, I always sleep with earplugs when I stay at hotels. And a night mask. And I brought those Breathe Right strip thingies just in case."

"That's because you're smart."

"And probably why I'm still single."

We took turns using the bathroom and changing into pajamas. His consisted of ratty basketball shorts and a tattered Seattle SuperSonics T-shirt. The pillows were delivered while I was washing up. Jon lined them up to form a wall down the middle of the bed.

Before I'd left New York, Hazel had messaged me:

If you actually wind up having sex and need to talk to someone about it, feel free to text me from the bathroom while Jon is sleeping. Although please, no details. No offense, but picturing you and Mossy having sex is kind of gross.

I should have snapped a photo of our little pillow wall and captioned it: *Birth control at its finest.*

"Juvenile, I know," he said.

"But good for peace of mind, I guess," I replied.

"Which side do you want?"

"I'm a middle-aged woman—the side closest to the bathroom."

He sat on the right side of the bed and unzipped his laptop case. I grabbed my own laptop and climbed on the other side, each of us propping a couple of pillows up and leaning against them. You know the phrase *ignoring the elephant in the room*? Well, that's what we were doing while we checked e-mails and scrolled through social media. Except the elephant was neon pink. With sprinkles. Wearing a beanie with propellers. Sitting on the bed between us. And yet, something about our conduct—sans elephant—was homey. A togetherness within the separateness.

Jon abruptly closed his laptop cover. "What are we doing?" he said. "We're here to hang out together, not with everyone else."

"We're spending plenty of time together," I said. "I'm OK with us taking an hour to ourselves and chilling out."

"It's not that I want to smother you; I just want these next few days to be about us. I don't want to share them with anyone else."

"I'm not sharing anything with anyone, Jon."

He still looked agitated as I peered at him.

"Do you not want people to know we're hanging out together?" I asked.

"Forget it," he said, and opened the laptop again. "You're right. I'm sorry. I didn't mean to—"

"Because I'm not going to act like we're doing something illicit."

"It's not that."

"Then what is it?" I leaned slightly forward, one knee up, one tucked in, and waited for his explanation. The overstretched neck of my tee had tilted *Flashdance*-style, and I caught him completely fixated on my bare shoulder. Like a child zoomed in on an ice-cream cone. It was the first time I'd ever seen lust in his eyes. Sure, we'd FaceTimed countless times, and he always appeared on my screen with a twinkling albeit pixilated smile for me, as did I for him, even when we'd been nothing more than friends. But to see him ogling me—how could I deny the adrenaline that surged through me? How could I deny that I *liked* it? How could I deny that I wanted him to see more? And that *I* wanted to see more. How naïve I had been to think baggy tees and sweats would suffice in detraction, and to think we were shallow enough for it to have mattered.

He averted his eyes the second he was found out, one second too late for him. What was it Hazel had said to me that day at Toast café? We were a great movie that everyone missed.

"Are you OK with turning out the light now?" asked Jon in what sounded like forced casualness or, worse, overpoliteness. "We both probably need to get some sleep."

I shut down my laptop, closed it, and returned it to its case. "Sure."

"You can keep the TV on low if you want."

"Nah, it's OK. I'm ready," I replied.

I went to the bathroom and applied a Breathe Right strip to my nose. God, I looked like an idiot. Reemerging to a dark room, I felt my way to the edge of the bed and crawled under the covers. Jon was already tucked in.

"Well, sweet dreams," I said.

"Same to you," he replied.

I inserted the earplugs.

We lay side by side, frozen. Speechless. As if one move or sound would collapse more than a wall of pillows.

For as long as I can remember, throughout my singlehood, every night I would close my eyes and imagine someone—one of my male characters, celebrity crushes, Frankie Farnsworth (who was my first boyfriend in the eighth grade who sold Mazdas now)—crawling into bed and kissing me. I'd watch it as if it were happening on a movie screen. He'd kiss me and put a hand to my cheek and whisper, *I want you*, breath hot, impatient. Last year, before closing my eyes, Jon had called. *Hey, Sage? What if this road trip is about more than kicks? What if it's about us exploring . . . possibilities?* And just like that, in the dark, his voice in my ear, I had closed my eyes and imagined him. Crawling into bed. Mounting me. Running his hand through my hair. Putting his lips on mine. Kissing me. Holding me. Touching me.

Just like I was imagining him now.

My only response to him that night had been a simple *Maybe*. But I knew it was too late. I'd let Jonathan Moss in. And once I let him in, I didn't want him to go.

And I had to finally admit to myself that I still didn't.

And yet, here we were, *sleeping together*. Pillow wall or not, we were fooling no one but ourselves when we insisted we weren't crossing a line.

Jon gently broke into my thoughts. "Sage?"

I removed the left earplug. "Yes?"

"In regard to the item on the questionnaire about the perfect day, here's the truth: any perfect day I were to have would include you as part of it. I just want you to know that."

My heart pounded as a flash of heat shot up my spine. "You too," I said.

I want you. Here. Now.

But I can't. We can't. Ever.

"Today was a good day, for the most part," he said.

"Yes, it was."

We were quiet again, but not for long.

I pulled out the other earplug.

"What did you mean when you said, 'I wanted to want this,' after you sent me the letter and we talked on the phone last year?" I asked.

He paused before answering. "I was fucked up, Sage. I know that's a cop-out excuse, but so much of my behavior revolved around my fear of what true love looked and felt like. You knew too much of the real me. You were in the hole with me when my marriage busted up. You saw and heard me weep. And you loved me anyway. No one's ever done that before. Not even my ex-wife. That scared the shit out of me. That's why I kept inviting you in and then shutting you out. I wanted to love you so badly, but I couldn't do it without learning to love and value and accept myself first. That's what my therapist—her name is Joy—taught me and helped me achieve."

I didn't want to continue, but something in me was pushing it out, along with the tears. "Do you know what it felt like? Like I'd spent all that time in the hole with you, only for you to climb out by stepping over and kicking dirt on me on your way out. I felt as if you didn't *value* me. As if I never meant anything to you, even as a friend. The one thing I'd never felt with you was worthless or inadequate. Not until that phone call. It felt the way it did when my father left. That's why it hurt so bad."

He returned to lying on his back. I heard a sniffle and a sob and realized he was crying as well.

"I'm so sorry," he said barely above a whisper. "It was *me* I felt that way about, not you."

I placed my hand palm up on one of the pillows separating us; he slipped his warm hand into mine, and we closed our fingers together.

"It made me so sad because no matter how angry I was at you, I never thought of you as worthless," I said. "Because you *aren't*. And I never wanted you to feel that way about yourself. I always wanted you to value you as much as I did."

"I do now." He squeezed my hand. "And you are the most valuable person in my life. When I was at the lowest point of unworthiness, you were the only one who treated me otherwise. I never doubted your sincerity because I knew you weren't just trying to make me feel better."

You are the most valuable person in my life. I've been complimented before. From readers: *You're my favorite writer.* From clients: *You're the best hairstylist I've ever had.* From Gaia: *You are so talented in so many things.* From teachers: *You've got potential.* From boyfriends: *You're so pretty.* But never had I been *valuable.* The word was heavy as gold, sterling as silver, glimmering like diamonds, precious as sapphires. No, not the word—its *meaning.* Its intention. Its origin.

I was a high achiever. Made good grades in high school. Edited the school magazine and wrote for the newspaper. Aced recital after recital. Won Best Artist in the senior class. Made the dean's list in college all four years. Went to cosmetology school and excelled faster than the rest of my class. Landed a job at one of the highest-grossing salons on Long Island. Became a bestselling novelist.

Yet no amount of five-star reviews, fifty-dollar tips, or certificates of achievement could make up for the fact that my father knew none of this. That he never saw my potential. That he never *valued* me enough to send a letter, show up at the school auditorium with a bouquet of roses, attend my graduations.

My error, I realized as my fingers interlocked with Jon's, clasped like a locket, was that I was trying to prove my worth by *doing* rather than *being*. As if setting the diamond in the ring was what determined its value, and not the diamond itself. That I was trying to prove my worth, period. I shouldn't have had to prove anything to anyone, least of all my father.

In the darkness of the room, I could finally see clearly all the times I'd tried to do the same in love relationships. If I really wanted it, I'd *work* for it. But no matter how good a lover I was, no matter how attractive my body was, no matter how perfectly I curled or straightened or colored my hair, no matter how well I cooked or fixed appliances or took care of my car, it wasn't enough. *I* wasn't enough.

But I was wrong.

With my friend Jonathan, I was always just *me*. And as a result, Jonathan saw. He knew. He accepted.

"You were my friend, Jon. I was never going to be anything but sincere."

But what about now? Now that I was aware, now that I stood to lose him again, would I fight to keep him? Would I still try to prove my worthiness? That's why friendship was easier, wasn't it? You didn't have to prove. You didn't have to do. You only needed to show up.

I needed to do things differently. I needed to *think* differently.

"I've missed you so much, Sage."

"Thank you for this," I said. "I needed it."

"So did I," he replied. A few moments later, he added, "I'm sorry I killed any feelings you had for me."

Those were the last words I'd said to him. I called and left the message on his voice mail: *You killed any feelings I ever had for you. You killed everything.* I'd regretted them ever since. For the first time I understood what Hazel meant when she said I went nuclear on him. And maybe, just maybe, the words were directed at the wrong person. Maybe they'd really been meant for my father.

"You didn't," I said.

Giving in to feelings for Jon was like the Grand Canyon. Vast and deep and dizzying. And dangerous. It required me to make a leap, one I desperately wanted to make.

But I still wasn't ready. Still afraid I'd crash and burn rather than land in his sturdy, steadfast, strong arms or, better yet, on my own two feet.

"You know I'll always care for you as a friend, right?" I asked.

He drew in and released what sounded like a defeated breath. "I know. And I'll always care for you."

My heart deflated much the way his breath did.

I released his hand and rested mine on my chest.

The pitch-black silence returned until I said, "Good night, Moss."

Neither of us spoke another word, and I lay awake more lonely than I ever did in my own empty bed.

CHAPTER THIRTEEN

December 31: New Year's Eve

I awoke as Jon did his best to quietly slip out of bed and use the bathroom. I leaned over to peek at the digital clock on the bedside table: 5:15 a.m.

He tiptoed out and was about to pull off the shorts he'd slept in when I piped up in a froggy voice, "You going to work out?"

He practically jumped. "Geezus, Sage, you scared the shit out of me."

"Sorry. So, are you?"

"I am. Want to join me?"

"I'm thinking about it."

"Then get your ass up, Merriweather," he said as he picked up a feather-filled brick from the pillow wall and tossed it at me.

I sat up. "Do *not* start a pillow fight with me, Mossy. I am the Queen of Pillow Fights. Just ask Gaia. She caved under my wrath every time. I will pillow-beat you into submission."

"You don't scare me," he said. "Now, are you going to get your lazy Long Island ass out of this bed and work out with me, or what?"

I demonstratively groaned and pushed the covers away. "Fine. Give me ten minutes." I crawled to the edge of the bed where he was standing, hopped off, and brushed past him to rustle through my suitcase for workout clothes, changing in the bathroom while he changed in the room. Fifteen minutes later, with teeth brushed, hair ponytailed, and dressed in yoga pants with a neon spandex racerback tank top under a T-shirt, I stepped into sneakers and said, "Let's go."

We left our room and turned the corner of the desolate, L-shaped hallway, where floor-to-ceiling windows revealed the dormant kidney-shaped swimming pool outside and, to our surprise, a side-by-side tennis and basketball court behind it.

Jon's eyes lit up. "Screw the workout room—let's play HORSE instead," he said.

"Seriously?" I said. "At this hour?"

"Why not? I've got a ball in the car."

"Who keeps a ball in the car?"

"I do. Because I'm awesome."

"Won't we wake people up?"

"It's a *hotel.*"

"Exactly. So you want to be one of those assholes?"

"I already am one of those assholes. Come on, all those times we said how much fun it would be to shoot hoops together . . . or are you scared of a little drubbin', Miss Pillow Fight Queen?"

Yet another thing Jonathan Moss and I had in common: a fierce competitive streak that neither of us liked to admit to ourselves, much less anyone else.

"Go get your ball," I said, rolling my eyes yet secretly excited.

He turned on his heel and practically jogged down the hall and out of sight while I waited for him. Ten minutes later he returned with a scruffy basketball, tossing it from hand to hand. He then shot it at me with force, and I caught it without flinching, my fingertips grazing the fading grip.

"So why do you keep a ball in the car?" I asked.

"I started a pickup game with some fellow former newspaper guys. Although technically it's not a pickup game if you plan it every week."

"When did you start?"

"Over the summer."

A.S. I thought. *After Sage.* I wondered what else had happened in the last twelve months that was new to me.

I hadn't played organized basketball since high school intramurals. I used to shoot baskets for fun in my early twenties as a way to blow off steam from studying in college, and tried again in my midthirties, only to find myself practically doubled over on the court, panting.

Jon and I exited a side door and ambled onto the asphalt, dribbling the ball and passing it to each other along the way.

"You have to allow me a bunch of practice throws," I said. "I haven't played in a good ten years, not to mention you've got over a foot on me. Plus, you know, we're old."

"And I suck," he said.

"You keep a ball in your car. And you play a weekly pickup game, organized or not. That doesn't connote sucking to me."

"One has nothing to do with the other."

I dribbled the ball in place and sent up a brick, wincing at the sound of the humiliating bonking off the rim.

"A good effort for a first shot in ten years," said Jon as he retrieved the ball, dribbled, and comfortably went in for a smooth layup.

"Oh my God, I hate you right now," I said.

He grinned. "Shall we wager on something? I think we should wager on something. You can't play HORSE and not wager on something."

I sneered. "Of course you want to bet. You know you're going to win, you cocky bastard."

His devilish grin turned sincere in an instant. "Sage, if there's anything I know about you, it's that you're good at just about everything you set your mind to. I wouldn't challenge you to a bet if I didn't think you'd give me a run for my money."

"You're just saying that to get me to bet."

He shook his head in exasperation, like I'd insulted him.

"What?"

"Forget it," he said.

"Forget the bet?"

"No, we're totally going to bet. I'll even let you come up with the wager."

I paused to think of something in which I stood a fair chance while he dribbled in place.

"How about loser has to cook the winner a meal when we get to Tacoma?"

"Sure, if you don't mind toast."

"Please," I said, "I know you. You'll toss anything into a slow cooker with some potatoes and Tabasco sauce."

"You're taking the easy way out," he said. "How about this: if I win, then tonight, at midnight, we do the look-in-each-other's-eyes thing for four minutes, just like the experiment."

My insides tremored with the terror you feel on a theme park ride. I hated those fucking rides.

"Why are you so adamant on doing this stupid falling-in-love experiment? We're not in a controlled laboratory environment. We already know each other's baggage. We have a history. And given how our friendship was already taken to the brink once, I don't know why you want to risk it again."

"Because I'm an idiot and a glutton for punishment. We'll take our glasses off when we do it so that it'll all be blurry, OK?"

"And if *I* win?" I asked.

"What do you want?" he asked.

Good question.

I stared blankly at the scuff marks on my sneakers while my brain performed a mental database search. And then it came to me.

You know that scene in *How the Grinch Stole Christmas* (I'm talking about the classic cartoon, not the Jim Carrey abomination), when the Grinch gets a "wonderful, awful idea" and his face completely crinkles up with evil? I didn't even have to look in a mirror to know my face was doing that.

"I want your Stratocaster."

Jon's smirk finally disappeared. "No fucking way."

Jonathan's 1965 Fender Stratocaster electric guitar with rock maple body and custom Clapton pickups and sunburst paint was more than a musical instrument—it was a masterful creation loved into being by the guitar gods. He didn't just play it. He *coddled* it. Like, sweet baby talk and kisses and Nigel Tufnel from *This Is Spinal Tap*: "Don't point at it." He'd spent an entire five-figure book advance on it, and I was the only person who didn't tell him he'd just frittered his money away on a midlife toy. In fact, I told him to shell out for the amplifier as well. After all, you couldn't play a Strat on some shitbox amp you got at Guitar Center. No, you had to go to Sweetwater for that, where the grown-up musicians buy their gear. Yes, I was a keyboardist, not a guitar player. At best, I'd dabbled with Gaia's acoustic guitar when I was a teenager, having taught myself the basics. But this was pure lust, I tell you. The '65 Stratocaster was the sound equivalent of a Havana cigar or Belgian chocolate. You could play scales on that guitar and I'd want to go to bed with you.

I nodded triumphantly; I'd just rattled Jonathan Moss.

"The four-minute gawk for your Strat. Now we got ourselves a fucking game of HORSE," I said, feeling rather cocky myself, and whisked the ball from him in a perfect John Stockton steal as I went in for a layup of my own—it ricocheted off the backboard and bounced on the rim, away from the net rather than through it, but much closer this time.

"You're on, Merriweather. Prepare your peepers, because you and I are going to give each other the eyeball once-over tonight."

"Yeah, that's so not romantic when you say it like that."

"Who's trying to be romantic? This is war."

Did he realize what we'd just done? Because I sure did. Jon and I had just leveraged the very things we were most terrified to lose.

And there was no guarantee either of us was going to win.

Chapter Fourteen

"Rock-paper-scissors to see who goes first?" I said.

Jon and I stood toe to toe on the court as we simultaneously counted out; we both dealt rocks. Typical.

We counted out a second time. Again, rocks.

"For fuck's sake!" he yelled.

A third count, and this time I dealt paper and he dealt scissors. I should have known. He gleefully cut into my hand with his index and middle fingers before gripping the ball and dribbling in for another layup. "That shot doesn't count, although it was a thing of beauty."

"So are you going to give me a break, or are we going to be making all jumpers from the three-point line?" I asked.

"I'll be fair," he said. "But let's change the rules a little bit. Every time one of us misses, the other one gets a letter. Otherwise, we'll be here all day."

"I thought those were the actual rules."

"Maybe they are. Maybe I'm messing with you."

"Maybe you don't want your ass kicked," I replied. He winked and pointed at me as conceding the first score to me.

He started from the paint, moved a few steps to the left of the free-throw line, and netted his first jump shot.

I'd gotten in at least a dozen practice shots (and made only one of them), but now it was time for the rubber to meet the road. Sort of. I moved to Jon's spot, mimed the arm motion of a jump shot, aimed my focus at the backboard, imagined one strum of the Stratocaster, and released the ball. Swish.

"Ha!" I exclaimed, jubilant. Even Jon looked impressed.

"Lucky first shot," he said.

"I work well when properly motivated," I said, momentarily forgetting that he had no qualms about dishing out his own psychological warfare.

"So do I," he said, and pointed two fingers to his eyes before redirecting them to mine. I shuddered.

He moved to the other side of the free-throw line, approximately the same distance from the basket as the previous position, and sent up another jumper. It bonked on the rim and off the backboard, but missed the basket.

"*Shit,*" he said. He found a stone and converted it to a piece of chalk, scratching a lowercase *T* on the court and adding the initials *JM* on the upper left quadrant and *SM* on the upper right. Then he carved an *H* under his initials in the lower left quadrant.

"This might be a quick game," I said, meeting the ball and dribbling it back to his location. I attempted the same focus as before, but my angle was completely off, and I bricked again. "*Blech,*" I said, as if I'd just tasted something rancid. Jon scratched an *H* under my initials.

"At least it wasn't an air ball," he said. "An air ball is way more pathetic."

Jon dribbled the ball to the free-throw line this time and released it without setting himself up.

Air ball.

He gave me a death glare. I stifled a giggle.

I dribbled to the free-throw line and aligned myself with the basket. *Be the free throw,* I silently recited. At the very nanosecond my fingers were about to release the ball, Jon spat out a "midnight" in a mock cough, resulting in an air ball of my own. He looked annoyingly satisfied, shit-eating grin and all.

"I see we're playing dirty," I said.

"No, we're playing cutthroat," he replied. "Dirty would be playing strip HORSE. We're now 'ho' to 'ho.' Wanna go for full-out 'hor'?"

"We're still talking basketball, right?" I said. "Because you never can tell in Vegas."

The quip pulled a laugh from him, prompting me to beam. Making Jonathan Moss laugh was still one of my favorite pastimes. It had been practically since day one, and was something I'd never quite gotten used to missing in all the months we'd not spoken to each other. Maybe it was the way he laughed, as if it was the funniest thing he'd ever heard. His laugh was contagious, even in print. Or maybe it was because he was so funny himself, and it was a feat not unlike impressing Burt Bacharach with a song you wrote.

"So hey, it's morning. Are you more mechanically inclined?" I asked, referring to a question we'd answered the day before: *If you could wake up with some new ability, what would it be?*

"Get me something to use a tool on and I'll let you know," he said, and quickly added, "That's not a euphemism."

He took his time testing out different angles and positions and distances before taking his next shot. "How about you?" he asked. "Are you more patient?"

"Just shoot the damn ball already," I retorted, as we broke into laughter almost before the joke even came out.

Laughing with Jon was an endorphin release.

"Walked right into that one," he said. As he settled on a position and was about to attempt the shot, he stopped and looked at me.

"Actually, I was thinking about it, and I want to change my answer. I'd like to wake up being fully compassionate."

I was equal parts moved and perplexed. "I think you're plenty compassionate, Jon. You stand up for those who need a voice with an innate understanding of why they need your voice, you understand that citizenship is the way to progress, and you care about outcomes."

"That's a different kind of compassionate," he said. "I wasn't compassionate when I was married. At least not to my wife, to whom I should have been more than to anyone else."

"Was she compassionate to you?" I asked.

He looked at the basketball regretfully. "No. If we were half as compassionate to each other when we were married as we became when we divorced, we probably wouldn't have gotten divorced in the first place." He bounced the ball hard. "Hindsight is a real bitch," he said, and hurled the ball at the hoop. It teasingly rolled around the rim and impotently fell off.

I picked up the ball and held it. "Remorse is compassion, I think. Doesn't matter if it's in hindsight." I approached him and leaned in. "Where's this all coming from? What brought this on?"

"I was thinking about our conversation last night. I knew that letter had hurt you, but I don't think I truly understood the ways and depth in which it did until then."

His admission was a reminder of the way in which texts and e-mails and FaceTime couldn't serve or sustain a relationship. If we wanted to build on this friendship, then how were we going to deal with the distance?

"I think the person you needed to show compassion to most was *you*. Both in and out of your marriage."

He looked at me, as if touched and impressed. "That's what my therapist said." He motioned me to where he was standing. "Your shot."

"How about we don't count that last one?" I said.

"Don't go soft on me now, Merriweather. There's a '65 Strat in it for you."

"Case in point," I said.

"Excuse me?"

"You just rejected my compassion."

"That's not compassion," he said. "That's sportsmanship. But OK. That one doesn't count." I transferred the ball to him in a bounce pass, and this time he banked the shot, smiling amiably.

I missed the next shot.

Jon and I each landed the next two sets of shots, and then he missed one and I missed one, sending me one letter away from losing the game and the bet.

"Tell you what, Squeaky, I'll let you pick out the next position."

"Don't do me any favors, Jonnie."

He made the shot despite my dig, and I bumped him out of the way with my arm and shoulder, as if the gesture were formidable. Given our significant height difference, it was cute at best.

"So what do you think will happen when we look into each other's eyes for four minutes at midnight?" he asked as I dribbled in place and aimed.

I dribbled again with determination, avoiding his glance. "I already told you—we're going to childishly giggle our asses off after ten seconds, say 'Screw this,' and go to sleep. If we're not already zonked out, that is. We were both asleep before nine thirty last night, I think."

"But tonight is New Year's Eve," he said. "It's illegal to go to sleep before midnight on New Year's Eve."

"I think my body is still on New York time, and as far as I'm concerned it will have already been 2017 for three hours by then. In fact, maybe we should do the eye thing at nine o'clock instead—that is, assuming you're going to win this game." I aimed for the backboard above the rim and sank the ball.

"Nice," he said, and applauded.

I turned to him. "What do *you* think is going to happen?"

He trotted over to me, stepped into my personal space, and said, "I think something phenomenal is going to happen."

I craned my neck to meet his eyes—the sunrise glistening and reflecting in them as if they were tiny lakes—and couldn't look away. Had I not caught myself, we might have accomplished those four minutes right there on the court.

"Whose turn is it?" I could hear my voice say, faint, as if I'd somehow stepped outside myself.

He released his gaze and attempted to spin the ball on his pointer finger, failing ridiculously. "Mine," he said.

He aimed and missed the shot.

That put us both at H-O-R-S.

We exchanged game faces. "Well, here we are," he said.

"Your Strat is going to love my living room," I said. "Lots of sunlight in there."

"How many hours 'til midnight?" he countered.

We dribbled and passed the ball back and forth to one another, whether to nervously stall or psych each other out, I honestly wasn't sure. We were back where we started when we began the game, ten feet from the hoop. I took the position.

"No matter what happens, this was a total blast," said Jon. "I'm so glad you agreed to come work out with me."

"It's a wonder I woke up."

"You didn't snore, by the way. I forgot to tell you that."

I was taken aback. "You were awake?"

"Since four."

Something about this disturbed me.

"I'm sorry, Jon. I didn't know."

"It's OK. No big deal."

"But you have to drive, what, eight hours today?"

"Probably closer to nine. I've driven longer with less sleep. I'm fine, Sage. Really. Go take your shot."

I aimed, but reconsidered. "You didn't snore either," I said to him.

"You wore earplugs," he reminded me. Jon glanced at his watch. "It's getting late. We've still got to shower—separately—and eat breakfast and get on the road. I don't know what to expect traffic-wise today. Take your best shot."

My heart pounded. My hands sweated. My vision blurred.

You know how in the movies, at that climactic moment when the game is on the line, and the ball—baseball, football, basketball, doesn't matter which one—moves in slow motion to its destination? I swear that happened the moment I released the ball. It soared silently in the pink sky, and Jon and I watched it, frame by frame, forming a perfect arc . . .

And then, unlike in the movies, it hit the backboard, bounced—no, *thudded*—on the rim, and fell off.

E. For eyes.

I lost.

"That was a fantastic game, Sage," said Jon, extending his fist to bump with mine. "Seriously, well done. Told you you'd give me a run for my money."

I fist-bumped him in a daze.

Completely unfazed, Jon took a swig from his water bottle and said, "Let's go get ready."

As we walked back into the hotel side by side, I asked, "Would you have really given me your Strat?"

"A bet's a bet," he said.

"But you knew you'd win, right?"

"How could I ever lose with you?" he said, sending my heartbeat right back into double time.

Chapter Fifteen

Following our game, we went back inside the hotel and took turns using the shower. As I was about to blow-dry my hair, Jon insisted on watching. "Novel research," he called it.

"Mossy, you put this in a novel and Joel will think you've given up. Which, let's face it, you have if you do."

"Still, I'm fascinated."

"Why?"

"Because you're a former hairstylist—you've got moves. And I'm envious." My gaze was immediately drawn to his receding hairline. Unruffled, he leaned against the bathroom doorway. "Go ahead, don't mind me."

I hadn't been watched since I gave haircut demonstrations at a trade show some five years ago. But Jon watching me felt more like I was taking a driver's exam. Naked. Despite the fact that I was dressed in jeans and a "Mad World" T-shirt. I removed the towel turban from my head to reveal the curly mop that was already frizzing. It was also in need of a touch-up, half an inch of gray hair peeking out at the roots.

"I always forget your hair is naturally curly," he said. "So what's first? Holy shit, you've got a lot of hairbrushes."

I eyed his reflection in the mirror. "Seriously, are you taking notes?"

He made a zip-locking gesture across his lips and said no more. From the array of products I'd set on the counter, I selected one, pumped a nickel-sized portion of the serum into my palm, and emulsified it in my hands as I ran them through my hair, taming the flyaways.

"You know, it looks really pretty the way it is right now. I don't know why you don't like it curly."

"Jonathan, we're never going to get out of here if I don't get this done."

He zipped his lips again.

Using a three-and-a-half-inch-diameter round brush, I straightened my hair section by section, keeping the blow-dryer way closer to the hair than one is supposed to. An occasional puff of steam coughed out of the dryer.

"It's all about tension," I said over the noise. "You want to keep the hair tight around the brush and pull little by little, letting the heat go through the brush."

"Hold the tension," he said with a clever smile that seemed to be hiding an inside joke.

When I needed two hands to handle the back sections and shoved the blow-dryer between my legs, close to my knees while it was still whirring, Jon winced.

"Whoa," he said, "that is one place I don't want to stick that thing."

"I'm not having a relationship with it."

He chuckled but seemed unconvinced. I pulled it out and aimed it in his direction like a gun, shooting him with a blast of hot air as he attempted to duck out of the way.

"Shit, Merriweather, that thing really is a weapon."

Twenty minutes, another brush, a flat iron, and two additional products later, I applied the finishing touches to what was now a smooth, shiny mane with merlot highlights that fell past my shoulders in layers.

I turned to him and struck a hair pose. "What do you think?"

A soft smile warmed his face. "Beautiful."

I couldn't ignore the flutter of my heart. "*That* is why I wear it this way. That look on your face. What you said. That's how it makes me *feel*. Beautiful. It's worth all the effort and expense. Curly is nice, but it doesn't make me feel like *this*."

"Sage, it's not the hair that makes you beautiful. It's *you*. You're beautiful no matter what. You know that, don't you?"

My heart inexplicably went from fluttery to vise grip in one nanosecond. "Look, you already beat my ass at HORSE and I'm doing the eye thing tonight, so no need to butter me up anymore."

Jon's demeanor changed just as quickly as he gave me a *what the fuck?* look. "I'd like to eat and get on the road before the turn of the calendar, so can we get a move on?"

~

We were on the road again around 8:30 a.m. Since leaving the hotel, I could barely draw more than one-syllable responses from him. Twenty minutes into both the drive and the discomfort, I peered at him.

"Do you want to continue the questionnaire?" I asked. Truth be told, given the agitation, I'd just as soon throw the damn thing out the window, but the silence was grating.

Jon shrugged. "If you want."

Lovely. As he set the cruise control, I removed the questionnaire from the glove box and unfolded it.

"What are we up to?" I asked, scanning the page.

"Why is it that every time I pay you a compliment, you think I'm either buttering you up or manipulating you?"

I did a double take. "What are you talking about?"

"I paid you an honest-to-God compliment on the court this morning—"

"After you taunted me," I interrupted.

"And in the bathroom, when I said you were beautiful, you pretty much shut me down."

"I was being sarcastic with you."

"It wasn't sarcasm. You were pissed."

"I think I know when I'm pissed," I said. "Like right now, for example. Right now, I'm pissed."

He shook his head. "Whatever, Merriweather."

"Don't 'whatever' me, Moss."

We covered about five miles, the hum of the car being the only sound between us. Nothing to look at except road and grass and sagebrush.

"What are we doing here?" I asked.

"What do you think?"

"I thought we were taking this road trip to renew our friendship and so you could come with me to my father's memorial."

"Do you trust me, Sage?"

"What does that have to do with anything?"

"Do you?"

I paused and sucked in a breath. "Jon, you wrote the most beautiful letter anyone has ever written me, in which you expressed your feelings and then completely bailed on me. And then, when I called you on it, you acted like you were *ashamed* of your feelings for me. Like you'd accidentally sent the letter to the wrong person or something—for all I know, you did—and it was all one big embarrassment."

He hit the steering wheel in frustration. "We're going to hash this out *again*?"

"Seeing as how you brought it up, yes, we are. You said some lovely things last night. But how am I supposed to trust when you say I'm pretty or talented or funny when you're liable to take it back at any moment?"

Jon wearily rubbed his eyes.

"You can't punish me forever," he said. "It's not fair to me or our friendship. I'm not your father."

I seethed. "How dare you bring up my father."

"How could I not? He's supposedly the reason you're taking this road trip with me."

"Supposedly?"

"Aside from last night, you've not mentioned him once."

I suddenly felt as if I'd just been caught plagiarizing. My face began to burn.

"I didn't realize that was a prerequisite."

"When your father died, you called me. You called *me*. And you cried and you were seeking something that would make you feel better about his abandonment. I agreed to go with you to his memorial. But I think deep down you already know you're not going to get what you want from that."

"You don't know anything about what I want!" I yelled.

"And you can't take it out on me. I'd never intended to leave. I just needed time."

"Maybe it wasn't your intention to leave, but you did. And you can't change that. If we get together, then I'm always going to be waiting for the other shoe to drop."

"Sage, your father left. And the other shoe already dropped last year, when I left too."

The words hung in the air, dangling over me, before plunging.

God, those freaking *home truths*—a phrase I'd read in a David Lodge novel years ago—he called it "a wounding mention of a person's weakness." They stunk like garbage.

I hated them as much as I hated Jon for giving voice to them.

And as they crashed down on me once more, sending me back to that ten-year-old girl's place of powerlessness, I went nuclear again.

"Forget it, Jon. Forget our friendship. Forget this stupid questionnaire. Forget midnight. It's over. *We're* over. The friendship has been over for a long time. It's never going to be the way it used to be. It can't."

He looked absolutely crushed. "Then what is this?"

"I have no idea."

Jon pulled over, killed the ignition, and unfastened his seat belt.

"What are you doing?" I barked.

"I need to step outside for a moment," he said.

"Are you—"

"Just leave me alone for a few minutes. Please."

He stepped outside, slammed the door, and stomped to the back of the SUV, where he restlessly paced. I watched him in the side-view mirror.

I thought I'd let it all go. I thought I'd made peace. I thought that when I'd finally accepted that Jon and I weren't going to be a couple, when I shamefully surrendered to Gaia's theory that I'd merely fallen in love with the idea of a relationship with Jonathan Moss, Author, and not Jon, when I'd finally submitted to the powerlessness of losing my best friend, I was over it.

I thought I was OK.

I wasn't.

It wasn't supposed to happen the way it happened. I'd never gotten over that. I'd never gotten over that letter. What had hurt most was that I'd let him in. All the way. Because as a friend I had nothing to lose. Or so I thought.

No one had ever gotten all the way in. It had been that way ever since my father walked out the door thirty-five years ago. He'd left everything behind—the birthday cards I'd made out of construction paper and glitter; the storybook I wrote about our miniature golf outing in which I scored three holes in one (I'd even designed a cover using a snapshot of us wearing matching Izod polo shirts, his blue and mine pink); Gaia's and my school portraits.

He didn't love me enough to stay. He wanted someone else.

The only thing my father had taken was my heart. And ol' fucked-up Freud was right. Prior to my father's leaving, I'd believed in romance and soul mates and true love. It was easy to write bestselling novels about those things because deep down, that ten-year-old still craved them to be truths. The refusal came from the inner adult who let me know in no uncertain terms: *Ain't. Gonna. Happen. At least not to you.* So I lived vicariously through my characters—at the end, love worked out for them. Every. Time. And I dated and had sex and boyfriends. But I had to protect the remainder of my heart, keep a vigilant watch over it. So I never let things get too serious. Thus, when those relationships had ended, regardless of who was responsible for ending it, I didn't grieve for long. I moved on as easily as I did when my literary agent or Joel passed on a manuscript.

I'd opened my heart all the way and showed it to Jon. It had been so easy. I wasn't even trying to shield it.

And he'd broken it.

He'd broken it wide open, in fact.

And since then, I couldn't quite sew it closed again.

Two minutes passed.

Five.

Ten.

Should I go out there?

After fifteen minutes, he opened the door and stepped back into the car.

"Here's the deal," he started. "Say the word, and I'll drive straight to LAX, get you on a plane, and we'll part ways once and for all. Or we'll keep driving, and tomorrow we'll attend your dad's memorial, arrive in Tacoma the day after, and you'll fly back on January third as planned. But if we do the latter, then by God we're going to fix this thing once and for all. Love is a decision, Sage. We can decide to be just friends after this trip, or more than friends, or nothing at all. But it's time to make a choice."

Love is a decision. When did he start talking like that? When did he start believing it? Was this what months of therapy had done for him? Had it made him more certain? Had it given him clarity and direction?

Here and now, we couldn't hide behind our written words or a computer screen or the miles of highway that separated us. We had to *relate* to one another.

The Jonathan Moss I'd been with since he picked me up from the airport in Phoenix was the guy with whom I'd spent countless hours FaceTiming and texting and chatting and e-mailing and sharing and laughing. He was generous. He was magnanimous. He was fun, and funny. He was caring. He was sensitive. He was the guy I'd always believed him to be.

He was my best friend.

He was also vulnerable, I realized.

Scariest of all, he was *available* this time. Not only physically, but also emotionally.

This road trip wasn't about going back to what our friendship was, but starting completely anew. Cleaning the slate. Dumping everything out (like in a grand canyon, for example) and telling new stories face-to-face this time, using a questionnaire to do so.

What was my decision going to be?

"I'm sorry, Jon," I said. "You were right. I've been blaming you for something that happened to me a long time ago. I didn't even realize it until now."

"I know I gave you a reason not to trust me in the past, but can you see things are different for me now? Can you see I'm even better than I was before?"

"I want to," I said, instantly flashing back to his explanation for why things had imploded between us: *I wanted to want it. But I just can't make it happen.* I suddenly understood what he meant. It wasn't about not being able to make it happen. It was about not being *ready* to. It was about being too damn terrified to jump out of the airplane and find that your parachute wouldn't open, or discovering that you'd jumped out alone when you thought someone else would be with you. So you didn't jump at all.

"Earlier, when you were doing your hair, you mentioned 'holding the tension,'" he said. "Joy used to tell me that regarding any situation I was in the process of working out. I think that's what we need to do while we work out this new way of relating to each other. Hold the tension."

"How?" I asked.

"Start by making a decision."

"It's not as easy as flipping a coin," I argued.

"You'd be surprised." He paused for a beat. "Here," he said, opening the armrest between us and pulling out a quarter. Heads, you decide to trust me; tails, you decide not to."

"Jon, that's—"

He blocked my objection with his hand. "Heads, you decide to trust me; tails, you don't. I'm going to flip it, and whatever you *want* it to land on is what you go with. Ready?"

He feebly tossed the quarter in what little space he had. And as it came down, I knew: I wanted to trust him. More than anything in the world.

He caught the coin, flipped it onto his arm, and kept it covered.

"Heads," I said.

"OK, then," he said, and tossed the coin over his shoulder without looking at it. "Heads it is."

I sat there, agog. Jon fastened his seat belt and started the car.

Chapter Sixteen

"So, do you still want to continue with the questionnaire?" I asked following our coin toss and after we resumed driving.

"Why wouldn't we?" asked Jon.

"May I remind you that the questionnaire was designed to determine whether two people can fall in love. And even though we've made up our own rules as we've gone along, I'm wondering if we should keep going. Or at least clarify what our purpose is in doing so."

"You promised to do the thing at midnight," he said. "I won that bet fair and square."

"I have every intention of keeping that promise."

"Seems pointless to do that if we haven't answered all the questions. Besides, aren't you even a little bit curious to see what happens at the end of it all? Or is falling in love with me such a horrid prospect?"

Quite the contrary.

"Has it occurred to you that maybe falling in love with *me* ain't no Macy's parade?" I countered. "I sleep with three blankets and a comforter on the bed—right through April. I take thirty-minute-long showers. I don't share dessert."

"I drink milk straight out of the carton."

"I liked the movie *Ishtar*."

He squinched his face as if he'd just smelled something foul. Then he volleyed with, "I use the combination shampoo and conditioner," to which I recoiled.

"And you admit that?"

"Proudly."

"Well, that settles it," I said. "We'll never fall in love."

"Nope," he replied. "Totally not compatible."

We said nothing more, yet each of us attempted to stifle smiles. Sometimes I was just downright smitten with Jonathan Moss. And when I gave in to that rather than the fear of being hurt again, the idea of it practically tickled me. But giving in had gotten me into trouble the first time, hadn't it?

I surrendered. "Let's keep going," I said.

The questionnaire was divided into three sets. We'd finished Set I just as we'd entered Vegas and still had most of Set II and all of Set III to complete if we were going to do the four-minute gaze at midnight. Thus, we blew through some of the questions either with little to no follow-up discussion or guessing each other's answers. We already knew, for example, that in response to number fourteen, my dream was to travel across Europe, and the reason I hadn't yet done it was a fear of flying across an ocean. Jon's dream was to build something, like a house, and what stopped him was fear of enormity. As with so many things, the day the depth of one's desire surpasses the depth of one's fear is always when one's life changes for the better.

The question begged for more, however: a metaphor of our present circumstances. Or, at least, my writer mind interpreted it as such. Why didn't Jon and I travel together one year ago? How had we gone from being certain we loved each other beyond friendship to being uncertain about whether love was even possible?

Fear of flying. Fear of enormity. Maybe the metaphor was already there.

We'd shared our responses to numbers seventeen and eighteen a year ago: Jon's best and worst memories were "the day I got married" and "the day my marriage was over." My best memory was one of the last days my family was together as a unit—Gaia, my mother, my father, and me—playing miniature golf together and going out for pancakes afterward; the worst was the day my father walked out the door and never came back.

But here and now, with hours and miles to cover, we unpacked those stories. Here I was, opening my heart to my friend Jon yet again because I'd decided to trust that he wasn't going to break it again.

Our responses to what we most value in a friendship were near identical: the ability to be one's most authentic self, and to be able to share openly and lovingly, without fear of judgment or rejection (or, I discovered, abandonment). But in response to the question after it, we had uncharacteristic difficulty articulating friendship in terms of a definition until we decided that what we valued and how we defined the word weren't all that different.

"Do you think we've been authentic with each other on this trip?" asked Jon.

"I think we've been trying too hard, whereas a year ago we didn't have to consciously think about it," I said.

"But we slid in comfortably in terms of the way we talk and joke around after not speaking to each other for most of the year. We've also been open and honest with each other, don't you think?"

"I didn't have a problem with trusting you when we were friends," I said. "And you called me out for not being open or honest about that. But we're working on it now. That's a good thing."

He was quiet, taking in what I'd just said.

"Do you regret having had feelings for me?" he asked.

"No," I said without pause. "When you look back on where we were in our lives, it was a logical progression for us. We couldn't have stopped it from happening no matter how hard we tried. The feelings weren't the problem. It was acting on them so impulsively that fucked us in the end. And then we made the colossal mistake every set of friends who've ever been in our position has ever made: we tried to pretend it never happened."

"I'm ashamed to say I regretted it for a while. Not the feelings; the way I behaved. I've never quite had your insight and wisdom with such things. At least not until I got into therapy."

My *insight and wisdom*?

"I'm the biggest liar there is, Jon."

"What do you mean?"

"I've made a career telling lies. I write about all these relationships in all their absurdity, but in the end they all work out, and people tell me I so 'get' it. But if that were the case, then why has no relationship of mine ever worked out? I mean, not even close. Hell, you were the longest long-term relationship I've ever had with a guy, and you and I never even had sex. Why is that, Jon?" I asked.

"Maybe you weren't with the right guys." He paused for a beat. "Although Joy says that's not the case. She called all my past relationships, including my marriage, 'cab rides.' Each ride was a part of my journey and taught me something. Doesn't mean they were wrong. Just that they weren't meant to last."

"That's a nice way of looking at it," I said.

Were we a cab ride too?

"You're the only woman in my life who never lacerated my heart, Sage. The only one. I'm so sorry I wasn't able to be the only man in your life who never lacerated yours."

My eyes welled up. "I'm sorry too."

He removed his hand from the steering wheel, as if looking to place it elsewhere—possibly on top of my own resting in my lap—but he had second thoughts.

I dabbed my eyes with a tissue and returned to the questions, the paper already worn with crinkles and creases and smudges.

"What roles do love and affection play in your life?" I read aloud.
We simultaneously burst into laughter.

We had been driving for almost five hours since leaving Las Vegas.
Traffic was at a minimum given that today was a holiday. We also managed to circumvent construction areas, thanks to Jon's having taken just about every route possible between Tacoma and Phoenix in the last ten years. Like me, Jon preferred driving to flying, although his reasons differed from mine. He'd done so much flying as a sports journalist that he saw it as something occupational rather than leisurely, even though it was a quicker and safer mode of travel, if not as convenient. But driving was time to see back roads and undeveloped land and ghost houses. Driving was *thinking* time. It was writing time. It was a time to sing out loud or live in his head or get to a destination as soon or as late as he wanted to. When he was driving alone, that is. It was all those things for me too.

We stopped in Bakersfield for lunch, but Jon requested we take it to go. I acquiesced, figuring he wanted to save time. However, instead of getting back on the highway going north, he entered the south ramp.

"What are you doing?" I asked.

"Taking a detour."

"Where?"

"You'll see," he said, poorly concealing a grin. "It's going to ruin the rest of our itinerary, but it'll be worth it."

Approximately two and a half hours later, we arrived at Pismo Beach.

"You needed to see the Pacific Ocean. Would have been a crime not to on this trip."

I leaned over and kissed him on the cheek. Invisible sparks popped and jumped all over my arms as I pulled away.

He opened the car door, removed his shoes and socks, and cuffed up his jeans. "Bring the questionnaire," he said. "We'll tackle at least one more."

I'd never seen the Pacific before. In a word, *blue*, like a sapphire. Jon said the sunnier the day, the brighter the blue. And freezing. The sand, however, was a warm blanket in contrast. Even in December.

We stood side by side while the waves broke and splashed our shins, as I squinted at the paper, even with sunglasses on, and said, "OK, here's a challenge: you have to say five nice things about me."

"That's all?" he asked. "It'll be hard to choose only five from so many."

I blushed. "I'll go first, then," I said with a wink, and he took the joke in stride.

When I didn't proceed immediately, Jon said sarcastically, "Take your time."

"I'm trying to think of the less obvious ones," I said.

"What are the obvious ones?"

"You know—freaking fabulous writer, god-awful funny, enviously well read, annoyingly intelligent . . ."

He seemed pleased, even though we'd exchanged those compliments repeatedly throughout the course of our friendship.

"That's only four," he pointed out.

"Better at math," I retorted. He cracked up.

"OK," he said. "For real. Let's come up with some stuff."

"OK," I started, and took in a breath. "First of all, you've been thoughtful with things like holding doors open and carrying my bags," I said. "I don't know if you're just doing that for me now or if that's a regular thing for you—and I don't mean that as a trust issue."

"No, that's a fair point," he said. "I admit I got complacent with Shannon. If there's anything I learned, it's that nothing kills a marriage faster than complacency. So it's something I'm being more conscious about. And not just with chivalrous things like holding doors.

I'm trying to better serve the people I care about in all kinds of ways without being subservient."

What an interesting notion, to be of service to someone you care about, even love. That is, when the proper boundaries were in place. I'd never thought of it that way.

I continued. "Two: You're a good listener. And you've always given me good advice."

He grinned. "Again, something I did very well in friendship, but was lousy at when it came to love relationships and my marriage."

"Why is that?" I asked. "I mean, why are the things that are so easy in friendship, like honesty and listening and sharing, so difficult in a love relationship?"

"People don't fear vulnerability in friendships. There's an alleged price to pay for those things in love. Perceived risks. But it's all a smoke screen."

"What is?"

"Vulnerability. The thing we're most frightened of happening already has. The thing we're really afraid of is that it will happen *again*."

Holy shit, ain't that the truth.

The sand pulled at my feet as the water receded, firmly implanting them. The realization sank in the same way. We put up all these walls and blinders and act like everything is fine to keep it from happening again—whatever "it" is. But all that does is keep you locked in the state of misery you're trying so hard to prevent.

I gazed at him, bewildered, as if trying to see right through to his thoughts.

"How'd you get so insightful?" I asked. "You've always been a deep guy, but you never used to talk like *this* before."

"Some guys get Ferraris when they hit midlife. I got answers."

I stared at the horizon on the ocean, feeling like a fool. I'd gotten answers too, I now realized, but I'd never paid attention to them.

"What's next?" asked Jon.

I pressed on. "Well . . ." I took a breath and collected my thoughts. "I know you already know this, but it's always been a biggie for me: you make me want to be a better writer. Still. Even with the last book I wrote, you were one of the few people I wanted to impress. You always are."

"I'm honored by that."

"Let's see, how many is that? Three?"

He nodded.

"OK. Four: I really admire that you got counseling. It's completely transformed you. No, that's not right. It's not that you're different. It's that you're more . . . I don't know. You're just *more*."

He beamed. "Thank you. It's the best thing I've ever done, and Joy is one of the best people I've ever had the privilege to know. She saved my life. Maybe not literally, but in terms of quality, definitely. And we're not done yet. It's an ongoing process."

I submitted to the urge to hug him. Just like at the airport, his arms tucked me in. His belly was soft, like resting your head on a pillow. As his hands moved in circles on my back, I closed my eyes and soaked in the warmth. Were it not for the three-hundred-some miles we still had to go, we might have stayed there all day. I certainly wanted to.

He seemingly thought the same thing and released me. "One more to go," he said.

"OK. Here's something I've never told you: your novels showcase an impressive vocabulary. That's an insecurity of mine, actually. I've never had a good vocabulary. Goes along with my insecurity about not being well read. I'm a creature of habit. When I was a kid I read all the Dr. Seuss books obsessively and repeatedly. Ditto for Judy Blume. And then my next favorite author, and the next, and next, and next. Hell, I've even read several Jonathan Moss books more than once."

"You have?" He was visibly touched.

I nodded. "*Bleacher Seats*. And *Oscar Wild*. I liked it even more than *OCD*."

OCD was Jonathan's breakout novel, the one that garnered attention in the indie publishing world and eventually from Joel, our acquisitions editor. It was about a television personality named Oscar Carmine Davis whose life is turned upside down when he gets evicted from the apartment he's lived in for thirty years. It was a bit of a dark comedy, and the sequel, *Oscar Wild*, took our hero even further out of his comfort zone.

"Thanks, Squeaky," he said. "Those were some lovely things you said."

You know how you feel inside when you give someone a gift they absolutely love? Not just any ol' gift, but one that means something special, and you knew it meant something special when you gave it to them. Yeah, I was feeling it.

"You're welcome," I said.

He took a breath and let out an "OK," signaling his turn. "Well, for starters, you have the most infectious smile of anyone I've ever known. Your eyes literally twinkle. Like, a dark room probably gets a little lighter when you smile in it."

And dammit, I couldn't help but emit a toothy grin at that moment.

"Second, your overall attitude toward life is nothing short of inspiring. No matter what you're up against, you make a point to live life on your terms. Not many people are able or willing to do that. And many times you went against the grain to do it."

Hadn't he done the same thing? We'd both given up secure careers to be full-time novelists. We'd both ridden the wave of e-books and social media that was mostly responsible for our successes. How had I gone against the grain? I asked him.

"You never settled for a relationship for the sake of being in one." Before I could respond, he added, "Not only that, but also your approach to life is one of love. You surround yourself with people you love. You've always found work you love. You take yourself to places you love." He gestured to the expanse of the Pacific Ocean spread out in front of us.

Was he really talking about *me*? Which was the false image—the way he saw me, or the way I did? Or was neither accurate? I certainly wanted to be what he was seeing.

He continued. "And you write love stories. Which leads me to the third thing . . ."

He paused demonstratively, deliberately keeping me in suspense.

"Tell me!" I demanded like an impatient child.

He grinned and acquiesced. "You know, you said you were the biggest liar because you wrote about things you think you haven't experienced, but not once have I ever read a Sage Merriweather novel and thought, 'Well, that was disingenuous.' All fiction writers are liars, Sage. Every last one of us. I'm not telling you anything you don't already know. You know the Picasso quote: 'Art is a lie that makes us realize the truth.' You've always told the truth in your books. You're a woman who loves deeply, and wants to be loved deeply in return. Every novel you've written has been an exploration of that. And perhaps you understand it better than anyone else because you relive it with every story you've told."

A wave—the kind made of breathtaking beauty that chokes your words and makes you place your hand on your heart to harness it—formed at the center of my chest, moved upward, and crested over me, from the inside out.

"I don't know if that's admirable, Jon," I said, still choked up yet recovering my voice. "I'm touched that you think it is. But isn't there something cowardly about sending your characters to do things you're too afraid to do yourself?"

"What have you been too afraid to do?"

Well, I'm scared shitless to look into your eyes tonight, for starters . . .

"Getting on a plane, traveling anywhere I can't take a blow-dryer, Internet dating—"

"You got on a plane two days ago. You're traveling up the country to places you've never been before. And you're doing it with a friend who broke your heart. That's pretty damn adventurous to me."

"It's not a bad story when you put it that way."

"It's a fucking great story," he said. He pressed on, leaving me no time to sit with my thoughts. "Fourth, I love how close you are to your mom and your sister. I know it was just the three of you for a long time. You're such a strong, powerful woman because of that experience."

"But I think it stunted me too. I don't know how to relate to men. I always thought they didn't know how to relate to me, but these last few days . . ." I trailed off.

"Most of my friends didn't really listen to me when I told them about the divorce. They tried to convince me to stay in my marriage because it was would save me money and hard feelings and God-wants-people-to-be-married bullshit and dating is a nightmare at our age and good luck finding a woman without kids. But you—you were the only person who told me it was time to listen to my heart. You were the only one who told me to love myself. And when you loved me exactly the way I was—because let's face it, Sage, you saw my lowest, most broken self—what did I do? I bolted. You scared the crap out of me because you were the only one who showed me to me, and I didn't like me. It takes a woman who knows herself and lives as authentically as you do to be able to do that."

I'd spent a lifetime in which the world in my head was as idyllic as Main Street, Sag Harbor, minus the minimum-wage workers at the mercy of the millionaires. I wrote love stories that made readers laugh and swoon and forget about the laundry and kids and bosses for a few hours. It made for a great career and paycheck, but that's about it. I knew I'd lived a charmed life, never having had to cope with cancer or abuse or poverty or migraines or war or discrimination or any of the hard-core shit that people go through.

How was that authentic living?

A feisty wave crashed so hard and close, it splashed us above my waist. Like being pelted with little ice cubes. I winced and screeched and wrung out the bottom of my shirt.

Opening doors? Vocabulary? My God, I sounded like a shallow ditz in comparison to the woman Jon just made me out to be.

"I don't know what to say," I said, my voice breaking on every word, barely louder than a whisper. "I'm just as flawed and terrified as the next person."

"Your flaws and your fears are all part of what makes you real. You put them on the page too."

"So does that make us more or less compatible?" I wondered out loud. It was the first time I speculated us as more than friends, and not in the past tense.

"Fifth . . ." he started. Had he not heard me? I didn't repeat the question.

"I thought that was five," I said.

He ignored me again. "Fifth is that you're good at HORSE. That's all."

Chapter Seventeen

"OK, so here's what we'll do," said Jon after we brushed away as much sand as we could and stepped back into Penelope, saying good-bye to Pismo Beach. "Forget Sacramento. For tonight, I mean. It's too far to drive. We'll go to San Jose, hopefully find a hotel, and ring in 2017 there. It's about three hours away."

"Sounds good to me," I said.

"From there we can go to your dad's memorial. Then we'll have to spend the night in Eugene or Salem, Oregon, but it'll still be a doable drive back to Tacoma the day after, and we can spend a little time in Portland. What do you think?"

We were getting closer. To midnight. To Sacramento and my father. To Tacoma.

We were getting closer.

"Sure," I said, fighting off a wave of wooziness. "And by the way, if you ever want me to take over the driving, just say the word."

"No one drives Penelope but me. Not even you."

"Oh really," I said in mock outrage. "What if we were married— and that's a big *if*," I interjected. "Are you saying even then I wouldn't be allowed to drive her? What if my car was in the shop or something?"

He had the same Pavlovian-esque response to *married* as I'd had to *hitched*, only now I saw what it looked like: a raise of the eyebrows. A flicker of light in the eyes. A failed suppression of a grin. We were couching these words in jokes and what-ifs, but every utterance of them was a sort of test, a poke, a lob. And yet I wasn't sure if we were testing ourselves or each other. If it was the latter, then we each continued to ignore the signal. Or, more specifically, refused to acknowledge it.

"Well, I suppose then I could make concessions for emergencies." After a beat, he said, "I like this hypothetical. So what other concessions would have to be made if we were married?"

A surge of current coursed through my blood, like getting a B12 shot. Screw testing. Now we were *playing*. But it was dangerous play. Kids with matches.

"We get separate bathrooms," I said. One match.

"We've been sharing OK so far, don't you think?" Two matches.

"One night in a hotel room doesn't equal a marriage," I said. "And trust me, you'd want it that way if you lived with all my stuff." Three. Each one getting hotter, closer to the skin.

"Good point," he said. "I thought you just didn't want to share a bathroom with a guy."

"Well, yeah. Obviously that too. Boys are gross."

He rolled his eyes. "Fine. Separate bathrooms. Penelope restrictions. Anything else?"

He was amused. But the little match flame dropped a spark as I began to ponder, and hence the fire that started: *What if Jonathan Moss and I were married?* A ticker tape of images scrolled before me, and none of dreamy wedding gowns or picturesque gazebos or ornate bouquets. No, the images were all about *being* together—trips to Yellowstone National Park and Madison Square Garden. Walking hand in hand down Main Street in Sag Harbor, splitting an ice-cream cone from Olaf's. Sharing a writing office, desks pushed together, facing each other. And rather than swooning over all the mushy-gushy romantic oohs and aahs, I felt contentment, as if we were already there.

But that contentment quickly turned to fear. If I wanted that—and hell, I've been wanting it all my life—then I was going to have to ask for it. No more what-ifs or hypotheticals or metaphors. I needed to *ask for it.* Clearly. Concisely. Definitively.

Instead, I defiantly lit another match. "I think it would be fun to cook together," I said.

He nodded his head. "Probably." After a beat, he added, "You know I did all the cooking in my marriage, right?"

Well. That snuffed the fire right out. And made me want to stop playing the game.

"Did you resent it?"

"Never. Most of the time I found it relaxing. Probably because it was just the two of us." He went on a tangent. "Thank God for that. I don't know how anyone gets through a divorce when children are involved. It's hellish enough when it's just the two of you. But with kids . . . parents must feel like they're shooting their kids straight in the heart. The ones that really care, anyway. I don't get the ones that yell and scream and bad-mouth each other in front of their kids."

I flashed back to my own parents' divorce. What I'd remembered most wasn't yelling and screaming, but *nothingness.* I remembered my father growing increasingly quiet around us, disengaging with our mom, no longer attending Gaia's and my piano recitals, returning home later and later from work. And then, one day, he was gone—left on a Saturday morning, returned the next day with a U-Haul, packed his things, said good-bye to Gaia and me, and moved into an apartment with Kathleen.

Did he ever stop to wonder what he left behind in that house when he drove away? Two dumbstruck, devastated kids who had no control over anything. A wife and mother who failed miserably at pretending everything was OK, and who could blame her for that? I remember watching him carrying his belongings out to the U-Haul, one at a time—a chest of drawers, music stands, cases of musical instruments, a file cabinet, clothes that didn't fit in suitcases. I *watched*—didn't go outside and lug everything back in, didn't block his path in protest, didn't cry or scream or hit.

I did *nothing*.

I asked a question. *What are you doing?*

Moving some things, he'd replied. To think of it now, his answer was so cowardly.

Are we moving too?

You're staying here with your mother.

Where are you going?

Out.

Out. Fucking *out*! Coward was too kind. Cruel.

Daddy . . .

Sage, I'm busy.

For crying out loud, why hadn't I *done* anything?

He married Kathleen one year later. And probably cheated on *her* too, although I couldn't possibly know. Based on the visits I made prior to their moving across the country when he retired, he never seemed blissfully happy with her, although they remained married. When I turned eighteen, I stopped visiting him on weekends and holidays, as per the joint custody agreement, which he rarely honored anyway. By age thirty, we were down to phone calls approximately once a month, most of them initiated by me. By forty, we were at e-mails when I wound down my career as a hairstylist and began my career as a novelist, and phone calls on birthdays, which he usually did a day late because he'd forgotten. This year I didn't even get a belated voice mail.

"I'm glad I never had kids either," I said. "Or got married, for that matter."

"Why?" asked Jon.

"I mean, there was a time when I wanted the big wedding, the kind TV shows save for sweeps week, and happily-ever-after and all that shit. But I got it out of my system when I wrote *Down the Aisle*."

Down the Aisle was my third novel, a romantic comedy of errors. Still my best seller by far.

"I loved that book," said Jon. "But you didn't answer my question. Why are you glad you never married or had kids?"

"Who needs a kid when I've got Erika? And I don't have to pay her college tuition."

"Sage," he said, scolding, demanding.

"Because look where it got my mom. And Gaia and me. And you."

"Is Gaia not happily married?"

I thought about Gaia and Kevin. After fifteen years of marriage, they still referred to each other with terms of endearment like *honey* and *sweetie*. They kissed and held hands in public. They were constantly laughing over the silliest of things. They also bickered over household chores and monthly bills and Kevin's playing too much golf and Gaia not being organized enough. Gaia had once confided that she and Kevin attended couples counseling on a regular basis.

I didn't know you were having those kinds of problems, I'd said.

We go to avoid those kinds of problems, she'd answered.

"I guess so," I said in response to Jon's question. "I certainly wouldn't call her miserable."

"You really don't think it's possible for you?"

I took a detour. "Do you want to get married again? I'm not proposing, but—"

He smiled. "I didn't think you were. And yes, I do. I think I knew, even while in the throes of my divorce, that I'd want to be married again someday. And not because of the institution or the fear of being alone. I *like* marriage. I'm not sure I can explain that, but I do. Getting my shit together only reinforced that it was something I wanted. What

I learned, however, was that I can't be dependent on my spouse to be the source of my happiness. It's something I need to give and maintain myself to bring to a marriage."

Was that where I had gone wrong all this time? I'd certainly lived on my own long enough and had enough crappy dates and breakups to know that I had to take care of myself. But what had I expected a marriage to bring me? I'd let go of happily-ever-after because the divorce statistics defied that at every turn. I also never bought into "you complete me," which was ultimately what Callie in *Down the Aisle* had learned.

Maybe it was that I had wanted something *from* it, rather than bringing something *to* it, regardless of what that "something" was. Maybe I'd had too many of the wrong expectations. Or that I'd had expectations to begin with.

Chapter Eighteen

Holy hell, those final questions got deep. Not to mention depressing.

Of those final five, number thirty-two, which asked to name a subject too dire for jokes, was the quickest and easiest to answer. In fact, we both said, practically in unison, "Sexual assault."

Number thirty-three proved tricky. As writers, we'd taken lots of opportunities in our work to say things we wouldn't or didn't have a chance to say otherwise. We thanked the kindness of strangers. We copped to wrongdoing. We told off exes or bullies.

"Tell me something you've never told *me*," I said.

Jon paused to consider his options.

"The scene in *Bleacher Seats* when Henry got the shit kicked out of him in the locker room? That was me when I was fourteen," he confessed. "I became a fierce competitor after that. It stopped being about *winning* and started being about *beating*, you know? It wasn't even about *playing*. It was about dominating."

"How did you overcome it?" I asked, before amending the phrasing: "*Did* you overcome it?"

"I did. Again, the magic word: therapy. Joy helped me see how I'd carried that pattern straight into my marriage. Every confrontation with Shannon was four quarters, nine rounds, pick your sports clock metaphor. And my objective was not only to win but also to crush her in the process. And it wasn't just fights. We could have been playing Scrabble or going grocery shopping."

"You've never been that way with me," I said. "Ever. Certainly not on this trip, while we were playing HORSE or when we fought."

"You've been the exception to a lot of things, Sage. You've got a competitive spirit, but you've also got boundaries. My ex-wife was just like me—she wanted to beat me at every turn. It attracted us to one another, and then it tore us apart. Had I known I was like this and taken care of it sooner, I probably wouldn't have married her. She would have exhausted me. She *did* exhaust me. As much as I exhausted her. But once you're able to see the pattern, changing it really isn't all that difficult; it's a matter of replacing a bad habit with a good one. Practice."

"Do you think you could have saved your marriage had you noticed and changed it sooner?" I asked.

"Not if she didn't change too."

"What if she had?"

"I don't know. Seems to me what you're really trying to figure out is if I *want* to go back and fix it now."

"I guess I am," I said.

"I don't want to be married to Shannon anymore." He looked at me. "Am I talking too much about my ex-wife?"

"I don't think so," I said. "You're sharing what you've learned from the experience. I think that's important. And you've not bad-mouthed her. But you've also not made her out to be a saint."

"I appreciate that."

"And I think the writer in me finds it interesting to learn about relationship dynamics. It's what attracted me to psychology as a major in college too. I've always been a good observer. Lousy participator, though," I said.

"I think you should give yourself a break," said Jon. "In a lot of ways you've been fortunate to be single all this time. It's given you the opportunity to learn how to live with and take care of yourself. It's taught you that you're OK no matter what."

I'd never thought of it that way before, especially *you're OK no matter what*. Being an observer of relationships allowed me to write good stories about them, I believed. Not having a family to support also allowed me to take the risk of quitting my former career without putting anyone else in jeopardy, and to write full time. But I don't think I was ever fully comfortable with the cost.

"And look what you're doing tomorrow," he continued. "You're attending the memorial of someone you haven't seen or talked to in years. And you're doing it for *you* rather than him, so you won't have to go through life with regret."

Not to mention this entire trip with you. I didn't want to regret not telling Jon the things I'd wanted him to know. I didn't want a life without Jonathan Moss in it.

I had yet to tell him that, though. *What the hell are you waiting for?*

"Thank you," I said.

"For what?"

"You know some things," I said, and smiled.

He smiled too. "What are friends for?"

CHAPTER NINETEEN

San Jose was in our sights. The air had turned mild yet still warm, with a breeze coming off the water. Traffic had thinned since we'd left the mayhem of Southern California behind. Jon and I were avoiding the final questions—they required the most depth and we were emotionally exhausted. Instead, we turned to a more superficial game of "How Many U.S. States Have You Been To?" After negotiating the criteria (layover in an airport doesn't count, even if you eat a meal; driving through a state without sightseeing counts; staying overnight without sightseeing also counts), Jon ran rings around me. As a former sports journalist, he'd traveled with all the Seattle teams—Mariners, Seahawks, SuperSonics—to just about every other major-league city. As for me, I'd mostly been to states within driving distance of my home in the Northeast, with the exception of Austin, Texas, and Chicago, Illinois, for writing conferences.

"Well, you're adding five more just on this trip alone," he said. "That's pretty sweet."

"Is there a city or state you've visited but want to go back to?" I asked.

"Madison, Wisconsin," he said.

"How come?"

"It's a nice place. Friendly. Scenic. Affordable."

"You saying you want to live there?"

"I'm saying that if I had another move in me, I'd consider it."

If he had another move in him? Was that a glimmer of hope? Or nothing more than a hypothetical? What other places would he "consider"?

I imagined what it would be like to live in Madison, Wisconsin— or Tacoma, Washington, or anywhere outside Long Island—with Jon. Buying a house, combining furniture, merging lives . . . Would we fight over leaving the toilet seat up? Would we each have our own office space? Would we live downtown or in the suburbs? Condo or colonial? Could it ever be home?

"What about you?" he asked.

"I don't know," I said. "Boston was pretty neat. Especially Harvard Square."

"You sound unconvinced," he said.

"What does *home* mean to you, Jon?"

He seemed thrown by the question, but I suspect it had more to do with the abruptness of the tangent.

"I think it's a state of mind more than a specific place," he said. "Obviously, we use it colloquially to mean whatever address or state we live in, but I think it means more than that."

"How so?"

"I have no desire to live in Phoenix ever again. But every time I go to visit my parents, I say, 'I'm going home.'"

"What about Tacoma?" I asked.

"It's more home than any other place I've ever lived. But my marriage? The house I lived in with Shannon all those years? I can see now how little that felt like home."

"But what's the *feeling* of it?"

Jon paused to consider his response.

"You described it to me once, when you wrote about Sag Harbor. Everything in its right place and time. Where you know and love yourself. The warmth of the sun, even if it's raining or twenty degrees. Fresh air, even if you're indoors. Where you hide nothing."

I remembered writing that to him when he asked me to describe Sag Harbor, and after he mentioned that he'd love to visit it someday, I half-jokingly sent him real estate listings.

"I can't picture feeling that way about any other place," I said. "Even the beauty of Pismo Beach didn't prompt me to pack my bags."

"You're limiting your experience if you're confining *home* to a physical place. Think about it. When was the last time you experienced all those things, regardless of where you were?"

I made a mental list: Writing. Listening to just about every band from the New Romantic era. Books. Reading in a library or coffee shop. Reading Jon's books.

"Remember when we had decided on this road trip the first time, we pitched the idea of each of us driving to meet at the midpoint of Tacoma and Port Jefferson?" I asked. "Back when we were still friends."

"We *are* still friends," he corrected. "And I do. Valley City, North Dakota. It's been more fun this way, don't you think?"

"Way more. Especially considering North Dakota is . . . well, North Dakota. I'm glad you asked me to do it."

"I'm glad you said yes. We'll hit downtown San Jose in about a half hour. And later tonight we'll ring in the New Year together. Not bad."

"You're still hell-bent on doing the four-minute fake-out?" I said.

"It's not a fake-out."

"You know, I read the original research study back when that *Times* article first came out. I didn't see anything about that part. I only saw the questionnaire and what seemed to me to be inconclusive test results."

"I confess I didn't read the original."

"That surprises me, Mr. Journalist Who Leaves Out No Detail."

"Maybe I've gotten to be a little bit of a romantic," he said in a way that made me blush and avert my glance.

"Well, for the sake of . . . I don't know, science? . . . we should finish the questionnaire, although this has been the most unscientific experiment ever," I said.

"Agreed," he said. "Although for someone who's so cynical and resistant, you're the one who keeps coming back to it."

I eyed him suspiciously. "What are you implying?"

"I'm not implying anything. I'm just making an observation."

"I just want to see it to the end," I said.

"Why?" he asked.

I opened my mouth, but my brain didn't deliver the words.

"Because . . ." I started, and waited. "Because I want to know how it ends."

An invisible *Aha!* jumped out, seemingly from the backseat, and poked me.

"Good," he said. "Me too."

"And we're still aiming for midnight?"

"Midnight makes for good storytelling."

"I wasn't aware we were going to tell anyone this story."

I didn't mean for the comment to sting, but I could tell it did.

"Let's start at eleven fifty-six," he said.

"Right. Because that's not dramatic at all."

Jon guffawed, which made me feel better. And making Jonathan Moss laugh never got old. In fact, if I didn't know any better, I'd say it felt a little like home.

Chapter Twenty

I was long overdue for a phone call with Hazel, which she confirmed by saying, "My god, Merriweather, you sure do know how to keep your friends in suspense," in lieu of a greeting. "So, tell me—what's Mossy like in the sack? No, wait—don't tell me. Ew."

"I have no clue," I said as I paced along the sidewalk outside the latest rest stop. "We haven't had the pleasure." No point in telling her about the pathetic pillow wall. Jon was on the other side of the parking lot making phone calls of his own. I felt a strange distance when we separated. So little had taken place in the last two days that we'd not shared. So few moments of privacy.

"Then why are you calling me? I mean, I'm happy to hear from you and glad you're alive, but what's up, if not Jonathan's—"

"Stop right there," I said.

"OK, sweetie pie. I'm focused on you. How are you, for reals?"

"Confused," I replied.

"What is there to be confused about?"

"My heart was broken by my best friend, and that makes me ambivalent to getting involved with him again."

"Sweetie, Jon loves you. He was in love with you before he even knew he was in love with you. He just needed to go through all the shit of getting divorced before he could be fully available to you. He had to stop being Shannon's husband and get back in touch with *Jonathan*."

Hazel's words entered me and coated my insides like hot chocolate, warming me from the inside out. But I still felt bound by the past. Why was it so hard to let go? Why are the things we want the most the same things we fear the most?

"So then, what do *I* need to do?"

"Start being honest with yourself, for one thing."

"About what?"

"About how you feel about him. 'Fess up. Take a risk. Be vulnerable. And I mean, really vulnerable. Like take-off-your-clothes-and-open-your-chest-and-expose-your-heart-so-that-it's-within-dead-aim-of-the-arrow. Metaphorically speaking, of course. And don't string Jon along either. You didn't like it very much when he did it to you."

"I am not stringing him along," I said. "At least, I don't want to. I just don't know if I want to be involved with him romantically."

"*Why?*" she asked.

"Because . . ." I paused, and my mind finished the sentence: *it's too hard.*

"We have a good friendship. We're finally mending it and it feels OK now. Why tear it up again?"

Hazel, chewing on what I guessed was a candy cane—she practically bought out Target's supply the day after Christmas every year—swallowed and said, "You know what you need?"

"What do I need?"

"You need a makeover."

"Thanks a lot."

"No. You and Jon need to, like, press a 'Reset' button, erase all the shit that went on this past year, and just . . . make it new."

"This isn't some *Doctor Who* episode," I said.

"OK—first, I'm going to completely forget that you said something so ignorant and stupid. Second, if this were a scenario in one of your novels, how would you resolve it?"

"I'd write a novel about Jewish cowboys instead. I think that's a highly underrated genre."

"Sage," she said like a disapproving parent. "Sage, Sage, Sage."

"Yes, ma'am," I said. "I'll be good."

In Nora Ephron's novel *Heartburn*, Rachel's therapist asked her why she has to turn everything into a story. Rachel's answer was: "Because if I tell the story, I control the version."

It's pretty much been my M.O. ever since. Hazel knew it.

"It's not just your story, Sage. It's yours and Mossy's. Stop trying to make it turn out the way *you* want it to and listen to the truth that wants to be told. And before you say, 'It's not that easy, Hazel'"—she imitated my voice to sound like a Muppet's—"it *is* that easy. Just call 'Plot twist!' and sit back."

I desperately tried to come up with a pithy retort but could do no better than "Why'd you make me sound like Bunsen Honeydew on downers?"

"Because I can't do a Long Island accent."

"I love you, Hazel."

"I love you too, Sage. Although I may have to rethink that if you don't start watching *Doctor Who*. Seriously. How could you be so lacking in your awesomeness?"

"Tell JT I said hi. And tell Kalvin I think he's been avoiding me."

"Kalvin is neck-deep in his manuscript and burying bodies by the dozen."

"Because nothing says 'Happy Holidays' like a serial killer," I said.

The moment I ended the call with Hazel, I texted that very sentiment to Kalvin, who responded with the smiling poop emoji, which was his way of telling me he loved me.

I headed back to Penelope, where Jon was waiting.

"Everything OK?" he asked.

"Peachy," I said. "Hazel says hi."

"So does Kalvin."

Interesting.

Chapter Twenty-One

I dropped my jaw when I entered the room Jon booked in San Jose: two queen-sized beds adorned with pristine fluffy duvets and pillows. A pair of matching upholstered chairs and a table in the corner for reading, or enjoying the sunlight, or a nice conversation with a friend. Original paintings of seascapes by regional artists. A floor-to-ceiling window showcasing the San Jose skyline. Bathroom complete with double sinks, walk-in shower for two, and soaker spa-jet tub with aromatherapy bath oils and rose-scented everything.

"Holy shit, Mossy—this room is nicer than my house."

"Mine too," he said.

"You didn't have to go all out."

"I wanted to. It's New Year's. And I'm taking you to Original Joe's for dinner. You'll love it."

I had forgotten that Jon had worked for the local paper as a sports editor over ten years earlier and thus knew the city well.

"I didn't bring anything nice to wear," I said. "Like, not even close." It had all been part of my be-sexually-unattractive plan, although now the notion seemed downright stupid. And despite resolving not to bring makeup, I had tossed the cosmetics bag into my suitcase at the last minute, even though I hadn't touched it throughout the duration of the trip.

"You'll be OK. Some jeans and flats and a nice top, and you'll be good to go."

"I like that you know 'flats,'" I said.

"I know lots of things," he replied, followed by a Groucho Marx eyebrow wiggle.

Yowza.

The closest I came to "a nice top" was an animal print V-neck shirt. I paired it with skinny jeans, Clark sandals, and a leather jacket. Jon announced for the third time that we needed to be at the restaurant, like, now, if we were going to get a table, especially for New Year's Eve.

"Sir, yes sir," I said with a salute. "You're a schedule freak, you know that?"

He approached me and stepped into my space, towering over and practically touching me as my pulse shot up and beads of sweat instantly materialized on my brow as I took in a breath—not fabric softener, but lavender; that's what he smelled like, and freshly cut grass—and I thought for sure he was about to kiss me. "Yes, I am," he said without the slightest touch of apology before he backed up, turned on his heel, and went to take a shower.

I was in need of a fan. Or an open freezer door to stand in front of.

When I emerged from the bathroom—hair coiffed in a French twist (slightly lopsided, but only a fellow hairstylist would notice), makeup painted to perfection, dressed and accessorized—Jon was sitting on the bed with his cell phone, scrolling through an article, when he picked his head up.

And dropped his phone.

The expression—equal parts awe and delight and . . . serene.

No. Not serene. *Content.*

I didn't think I'd ever seen it before, on him or any other man. Or maybe I'd just never paid attention. My heartbeat thumped and throbbed like a bass drum.

He stood up and, as if catching himself in midair without anything to hold on to, fumbled and fidgeted and grabbed his phone from the floor.

I caught a whiff of cologne as he approached me. He wore taupe slacks with a black button-down cotton shirt and shoes. Damn. Mossy cleaned up good.

Every step toward me, every second of nonverbal communication, set off a cacophony of snaps, crackles, and pops throughout my body. Yes, I was a human bowl of Rice Krispies.

"You are the most beautiful woman I've ever known, Sage."

Every firework and function within me stood still.

"Lipstick does wonders," I joked in an effort to desensitize the moment.

Jon wasn't having it. "I'm serious," he said. "And I'm not talking about lipstick. You're beautiful when you're makeup-free, or dressed in pajamas, or even when your hair is dripping wet."

"Thank you," I replied, bashful, bewildered, breathless.

He took a step back, and his expression turned inquisitive, almost childlike. "Do you find me physically attractive, Sage?"

Despite writing about pretty boys with sculpted abs in my novels, in real life the beauty I'd found in men always went beyond skin-deep. Smart was sexy. Funny was fetching. Talent was tasty. Jon was all those and more. Thoughtful and caring and self-aware.

But I wondered if I was more superficial than I insisted to the contrary.

I'd never told him he was handsome. Had never alluded to his looks throughout the duration of our friendship. He was never going to have the six-pack abs of Ryan Gosling, or the sculpted facial features of Rob Lowe, or the delectable voice of Anthony Hopkins. But he was taking care of himself physically and emotionally. It didn't change the fact that he stirred something in me; something sexual and soft and satisfying.

"Jon," I said softly, taking a few steps back. "We can't."

"I'm just asking a question."

"You're putting me on the spot," I said.

His face went from wounded to resigned as he said, "You're right. I shouldn't have."

I felt like a total shitheel.

He shook off any traces of hurt, took me by the shoulders, and gently spun me around. "Looks OK to me," he said. I thought I heard him inhale, as if to catch the scent of me.

"What does?"

"The back of your hair. I knew you'd ask."

Shit. Why did he have to be so . . . so *Jonathan*?

He swung me around again and took a few steps back.

"Thanks," I said, avoiding eye contact. I clutched my purse from the bed, draped the jacket around my shoulders, and asked, "Ready?"

"Are you?" he replied.

"For dinner, yes," I said. I fought every impulse to burst into tears.

He smiled, linked my arm, and escorted me out the door.

～

The Italian restaurant and bar Original Joe's was packed—a corner location in the heart of downtown—yet cozy and vibrant. After we were seated, Jon confessed that he had phoned the manager, not Kalvin, while I was chatting with Hazel, and called in a favor to make sure we got a table.

It occurred to me that this could be construed as our first date.

Screw *construed*. It *was* our first date. He knew it. I knew it. Copping to it would make the shit real.

But how much more real did we need before we would cop to it? Maybe we were waiting until midnight, when coaches turned back into pumpkins. Or was it the other way around in this instance?

The server delivered the drinks as I sized up the final question. "So now one of us has to disclose a personal problem and ask the other for some help solving it," I said.

He looked at his menu a bit too studiously.

"Do you want to go first?" I asked. "You should go first, because I can't think of anything right now."

"Very well." He took a pull from his Jack and Coke and set the thick glass down gently. I waived the no-alcohol rule on the condition that it was his only drink for the night—and even considered ordering one myself. Lowered inhibitions were tempting, at best. Perhaps even daring. At worst, dangerous.

Besides, we'd already trashed Rule Number One. And the rules of the questionnaire. Deliberately. Consciously. And it was New Year's Eve.

"OK," he started. "I'm going to switch things up a bit here."

I straightened my posture in anticipation.

"Suppose our friendship had never been compromised. Suppose I told you I wanted to rekindle a potential romance with a female friend from whom I'd been estranged. How would you advise me?"

Every muscle tightened as the blood started coursing and my breastbone rattled. I knew what he was doing. He wasn't waiting on me anymore. It was like walking through a Halloween haunted house, knowing a pair of bony hands were going to reach out from the darkness and grab you at any second, yet you keep taking one more step, trying to be prepared, holding your breath and gripping yourself . . .

Just play along, I thought. *Play along and you'll get through it.* Although my next thought, in Jon's voice, was: *It's not a game, Sage.*

I ignored his inner voice. "Assuming you'd already been involved with the friend?" I asked.

"Assuming we'd considered it but never moved on it," he answered. "Also assuming I was already divorced and never wigged out."

"So it's not so much *re*kindling as . . . well, kindling."

Another step. Waiting for those hands. Yeah. My strategy was so not working. Every one of my pulse points was sprinting.

"I guess so, yeah," he said.

I fixed my gaze out the window, as if a passerby outside would deliver the response.

"I'd probably pump you for more details, but ultimately I'd tell you to go for it," I finally said.

Tell him for real, you idiot! I wanted to. I wanted to so badly.

He perked up and raised the stakes. "OK, so here's another what-if: What if one of *your* female friends told you that a male friend with whom she has a complicated past resurfaced and has lingering feelings for her, and she's considering her options? How would you advise her?"

Again I looked to the window and the pedestrians. I wanted to be on the other side. In every way.

"I would tell her to move forward and forget the other guy. If it didn't work out the first time, then chances are it won't the second time, and why mess up something that's already going well?"

Jon, bewildered, asked, "Why would you encourage me but discourage a female friend?"

"In your case, I want you to be happy, to go for what you want. In the other scenario, with that limited information, the woman just seems to be too likely to get hurt. I guess I want to protect her."

Jon stroked his beard with his thumb and forefingers like a TV detective, uttering, "Very interesting."

Before he could pose another what-if, I jumped in. I needed control, dammit. "OK, what about you? What if one of your buddies presented your scenario to you? How would you advise him?"

Jon didn't even take a moment to consider his answer. "I'd probably tell him to wait and see how the relationship played out. But if he didn't want to wait, then I'd tell him to be completely honest with his intentions, heart wide open, and release all hopes and desires and expectations about the outcome."

Never had we danced around an issue the way we were both jitterbugging right now. Which only confirmed how much we had to lose this time.

And yet I kept right on sidestepping. "Honest with whom—himself, or his female friend?"

"Both, I guess."

I looked at him earnestly. "Is that what *you* are doing right now?"

"We're not talking about me," he said. "We're just doing what-ifs."

Now I was getting antsy. Impatient. "So what if *I* came to you as a friend, yada yada yada . . . How would you advise *me*?" I asked.

He took another pull of the Jack and Coke and let the liquid linger before putting the glass down and swallowing, not once averting his gaze from me, which unnerved me to no end. I leaned forward, hands gripping the sides of my chair, feet digging into the floor. Waiting.

"I'd tell you to do the same thing we did earlier in the car: flip a coin."

"Seriously?"

"Yeah."

"That's it? Flip a fucking coin?"

"Absolutely. Call it in the air, without giving yourself a chance to think about it. And then screw where it lands. Whatever you called is what you wanted all along."

"That's massively oversimplifying the problem, not to mention my feelings. Or anyone's feelings, for that matter."

"On the contrary, we're the ones who complicate everything by weighing everything out and scrutinizing every detail and investing too much in how the other person is going to feel and react, when really we have no control or responsibility for all that shit to begin with."

"I am not flipping a coin, Jon."

"OK," he said. "Like I said, we're just doing what-ifs."

"Are we?" I asked, pulling the jacket closed without slipping my arms into the sleeves. I wanted off the dance floor. Off the what-ifs and the scripts and the contrived questions. "The marriage hypotheticals, this 'advice' . . . What are we really doing?"

"You tell me," he said, an edge to his voice.

We were back on the basketball court, one on one. Only we weren't getting one shot each this time. We were battling for the ball as well as the basket.

"Let's tackle the question. No what-ifs. Give me an honest-to-God problem and ask for my advice," I said.

Jon looked away, seemingly contemplating diving out the window, before returning his gaze to me. He took one more swig of the Jack and Coke, set the glass down, and took a deep breath.

"OK." He exhaled. "Here goes."

I braced myself.

"I'm in love with you, Sage."

Bam. There it was. No more cryptic messages. No more dribbling or dancing around it. And there was the arrow straight to the heart. Bull's-eye. I put my hand to my chest, as if to keep my heart from falling out.

"I've always loved you," said Jon. He fully leaned forward in his chair, as if the table weren't there. "I loved our friendship, I loved the possibility of us, and now, having spent this time with you, I just *know*. But I'm not sure how you feel about me, if too much damage has been done to make a second chance possible, or even successful, or if you're ready. So I'm asking you to advise me on whether I should take any more steps to pursue a love relationship with you, or completely surrender that and instead continue to repair and strengthen the awesome friendship we've always had. And I don't know any better foundation for love than friendship."

God, he was completely wide open. As if I could see everything inside him. He looked frightened. But he also looked strong. He looked ready. He looked *powerful*. Seeing him that way both mesmerized and terrified me.

I sat there, stupefied. "I meant, like, ask me advice on whether you should get a hair weave."

He reflexively put a hand up to his bald spot but remained steadfast otherwise and waited for me to say something less flip. Before I could further reply, the server returned to take our orders. We'd forgotten to look at the menus, but rather than ask for extra time, we hastily perused and ordered on the spot—Jon, the veal piccata; me, the eggplant parmigiana. Although truthfully, the news flash Jon had just delivered rendered eating obsolete despite the hunger pangs.

After the server left, Jon looked at me intently and waited for my response.

I couldn't avoid the question—or the reality—anymore.

I stared out the window for a seemingly long time. The street wasn't speaking to me this time. I was on my own.

"I don't know how to advise you," I finally replied.

"Do you really not know, or are you too afraid of hurting my feelings?"

"I'm . . ." The words stuck in my throat as puddles flooded my tear ducts. "I'm just so scared, Jon."

Jon took my hand and delicately brushed my thumb with his own. "I know," he said.

"What should I do?"

"Look at these last two days we've spent. Look how we slipped back into our groove. Look how comfortable we are. Look how we've been able to communicate and work through our problems. You can tell me anything, Sage. *Anything*. You can be yourself. I'll never stomp on your heart again."

"Don't say *never*," I retorted. "Don't ever promise something you have no certainty of honoring. You may think you're certain of it now, but you just don't know a year from now, or five or ten or fifteen years from now. After all, you promised Shannon you'd spend the rest of your life with her."

He seemed struck by this notion, but absorbed it.

"I'm telling you this as a friend," I said, because I realized I was.

I looked directly at him. "You're my best friend. You and Hazel and Kalvin. But especially you. And . . ."

He waited for me to finish, but it was as if the power cord to my brain had been yanked out, rendering me unable to put together another thought, sentence, feeling.

Perhaps he surmised that my inability to answer was the answer itself: *And . . . I want us to keep on being friends.*

But it wasn't.

"In that case, let's not go ahead with the four minutes," he said, more resigned than defeated, albeit disappointed.

"But . . . what about the bet?" I asked.

"There's no point to it now. Knowing what I know now, it would be wrong to force you to do something you were opposed to all along. I need to respect that."

"I'm sorry," I said, my voice breaking.

"It's OK," he said. "Really, Sage, it is."

We barely spoke throughout the rest of dinner, and I couldn't shake off the sadness that had crashed over me. Yet a strange kind of calm had also settled between us, allowing the silence, even welcoming it so that by the time dessert arrived, we'd regrouped and found our way back to one another.

Correction: we didn't find our way back. We were there all along. And knowing that made everything a little bit better.

But not better enough.

CHAPTER TWENTY-TWO

Despite the intense completion of the questionnaire, Jon and I managed to get through dinner with talk about book sales and speculating on Bellevue Pages' personnel changes and the latest in analytics. And although the gaudy elephant that had been in our Las Vegas bed now invited itself to dinner, we left Original Joe's having pushed it out of our sights and minds.

"So I have an idea," said Jon as we walked down the San Jose streets. "Given that you're a New Yorker and you don't believe the New Year begins until the ball drops in Times Square—"

"That's not true," I interrupted.

"Oh no? I probably still have the text you sent me last year in which you said, and I quote: 'Doesn't matter what happens in the rest of the world. The New Year doesn't happen until the ball drops in Times Square.' I then called you a snob but still offered a midnight kiss."

"I should know to never go on the record with a journalist. Even a former one."

"Righty-o. Anyway, I figured we could find someplace to watch the ball drop and then head back to the hotel. What do you think?"

"Might as well," I said. "Why not watch in the hotel room?"

"Nah, I know a place nearby. I'm sure the ball drop is being live-streamed. We'll find it on my phone."

I slid on my jacket, zipped it, and crossed my arms; the temperature had dropped a bit since sunset. Jon led us to what he called "the square"—a courtyard with some grassy lawns and a fountain. We sat near the fountain and he found a live-streamed broadcast at five minutes to nine. At 8:58:50, we huddled close to the smartphone and witnessed the blingy, kaleidoscopic Waterford crystal and LED-lit orb descend onto the 2017 sign, triggering a confetti blizzard and drunken kisses across Times Square. Another chill ran through me, climate having nothing to do with it. For better or for worse, I was a New Yorker. Stick me in the underbelly of the beast and I'd fall victim to my own cowardice and naïveté, yet I still felt a kinship with the city and its skyscraper forest. But *Long Island*—wrapped in water, rural vineyards in the east, urban sprawl in the west, crowded and diverse and expensive and hectic and charming and deceptive and suburban and on the edge of the universe—that was where I lived. No imagination. The real deal. Home.

And yet here I was on the opposite coast, surrounded by city streets, fine dining, bodies of water looming not too far away, and a plethora of people, wondering whether I was really so remote.

I didn't even realize that I'd clasped Jon's hand until he squeezed it and said softly, "Happy New Year, Squeaky."

I met his eyes and replied, just as softly, "Happy New Year."

We stood inches apart at attention like soldiers, shoulders square, chest out, stomachs sucked in. Our eyes locked in, and I began at the surface. The color of his irises: almost purple in twilight, a reflection of the sky. The size of his pupils: black spots yet still sparkling, a reflection of the sea. The length of his flaxen lashes: long and straight, like little fan paintbrushes. The shape of his brows: perfectly aligned with the contour of his eyes, yet not too curved or arched.

I counted the number of times he blinked, which made me conscious of my own blinking, but only for a few seconds.

And then . . .

Something stirred within me as Jon's eyes began to glow—not like cat's eyes or some kind of extraterrestrial's, but like soft candlelight. Ambient.

It was as if I could see . . . *stories.*

The firsts of our lives before we met—first kiss, sex, rock concert, broken heart, publishing rejection, and royalty check. The bests and worsts. *Our* stories, beginning with the day we met at the party in New York City, to when we sat by a fountain in San Jose and watched the ball drop. All the stories we'd told each other in the car these last two days.

It was a story of *us.* Jonathan and Sage. Moss and Merriweather.

And it was a love story.

I made a living writing love stories. Not just of the romantic comedy kind. I also wrote them between parents and children, pets and companions, and friends. I loved a good love story. The journey was what made a love story great. The *relationship.* The back and forth, give-and-take, kindness and appreciation, generosity and trust. Love stories, or the relationships that told them, weren't about perfection. They were about acceptance. They were about struggle, but not a tug-of-war or hamster-wheel type of struggle. The kind of struggle a caterpillar undergoes to become a butterfly. Or like gardening. Daily maintenance. Attention. Presence.

Holding the tension.

Jon and I had been caterpillars one year ago. Our mistake was that we thought we could fly as caterpillars. All this time apart, we'd been in our cocoons.

Look how we slipped back into our groove. Look how comfortable we are. Look how we've been able to communicate and work through our problems. You can tell me anything, Sage. Anything. You can be yourself.

We emerged as magnificent, dazzling monarch butterflies.

"Sage," Jon uttered, his voice sounding distant, ethereal. He took my hand.

My eyes felt wet.

"Sage," he said more emphatically.

I answered with a faint murmur.

"You OK?" he asked. "Maybe we should walk for a bit."

"Sure," I said, dazed.

We were in desperate need of a conversation while we walked, except we didn't utter a sound. If we were supposed to talk about what had just taken place, then neither of us volunteered to put that subject on the table. Even if I did, I couldn't articulate the experience.

But *something* had happened.

I felt off balance. Like I was back at the Grand Canyon, looking over the edge. I stopped in my tracks and took hold of Jon's arm. He steadied me and placed a hand on my back and made soothing circles. And once again I looked into the eyes that had transfixed me, taken me on a trip inward, and found my friend. Always, first and foremost, he'd been my friend, and still was. I wanted to collapse myself into that friendship because it had always been the safest place to be. But now I wanted—no, *needed*—to go deeper. I regained my balance so we continued walking.

When we reached Penelope, Jon unlocked the door and I stepped in. We both sat still and silent. The key in the ignition, dangling, waiting.

"Jon, what happened back there, when we were looking at each other?"

He shifted in his seat and stared at the steering wheel. "I don't know," he said.

"That's it? You really don't know? Or you can't explain it?"

He didn't answer.

"Or maybe you can and you don't want to," I suggested. He didn't respond. "What was supposed to happen?"

"None of this went the way I expected it to," he started. "The road trip, the questionnaire, tonight . . ."

"Maybe it was a mistake to expect anything," I said.

He furrowed his brows and looked away for a moment, as if disoriented. "Shit," he muttered.

"I didn't mean that in a judgmental way," I said, and placed my hand on his. He neither held on nor pulled away. Just wore an expression of hopelessness.

"I know," he replied. "Let's just go back to the hotel." He turned the key and retreated.

Back in the room, I kicked off my shoes, sat on the bed I'd claimed earlier, and clicked on the TV. Jon washed up and changed into pajamas in the bathroom, crawled into his bed, and rolled over, pulling the covers up to hide the light.

Nothing. Not even a "Good night, Merriweather." Hell, it wasn't even ten thirty yet.

I turned out the light, washed up and changed in the bathroom, and crawled into my own bed. After watching a *Twilight Zone* episode with the sound muted, I clicked off the TV and pulled up the covers.

Another thirty minutes later, Jon still wasn't sleeping. I could tell from his breathing.

One year ago on this date, I'd put on the red plaid flannel pajamas my mom gave me for Christmas, parked on my couch, and zonked out watching the *Twilight Zone* marathon on TV, avoiding all forms of social interaction. It was a far cry from where I'd thought I would be and from what I thought I'd be wearing—in a swanky hotel (or, more specifically, in a *bed* in said swanky hotel) with Jon, scantily clad in satin black bikini bottoms with the words "Happy New Year" scripted in silver on the butt and a camisole. I'd bought a card that said something to the effect of "New Year, New Dreams," and had planned to bring the bottle of champagne he had sent me after *Down the Aisle* hit a hundred thousand sales.

Instead, New Year's Eve sucked last year.

Afterward, I'd returned the unused lingerie and dropped the card into the recycling bin. Poured the champagne down the sink. In the months that followed, I picked myself up and dusted myself off. I wrote. I walked. I spent time with friends and Gaia and my mom. I saved money.

And I concluded that underwear with writing on the butt is bad for any occasion.

I thought I'd recovered this year. Thought I was happy. But in actuality I'd spent most of it, I now realized, on autopilot.

This year, there was no booze, no card, and no sexy underwear. In the process of writing a novel, an author can sometimes get stuck in the swampy middle—the story lags, the characters have no place to go, the writer can't see her way out. How could I write myself out of this?

I replayed every moment that had occurred since stepping off the plane and into his arms two days ago. Reviewed every gesture, every exchanged glance, every spoken word. Right up to that moment the ball dropped and we looked into each other's eyes—spontaneously. No timer set to four minutes, no contrived start and stop. No note taking or analyzing or recording of data.

I fell in love with Jonathan Moss. Not on paper. Not through words on a screen or in a book. Not because of what-ifs. I fell in love with the man who brought me coffee, showed me where he lived, took me to the ocean, and opened his heart. A man who wasn't responsible for my happiness and wasn't asking me to be responsible for his.

The digital clock glowed 11:46.

"Are you awake?" Jon called out.

"Yes," I replied.

"My therapist told me something a few months ago: 'If you offer someone your love for the right reasons and with the right intention, you can't lose.' It took me a long time to fully understand what that meant."

"What does it mean?"

"Well, regarding this situation—"

"Which situation?"

"Yours and mine—what happened tonight . . . it means that my own purity of heart and intent were all I needed, and I didn't need a particular outcome. But I wasn't ready to trust that. I bet all my chips on this questionnaire and looking into each other's eyes, and expected it to undo everything that happened last year to take us to a whole new level. All it did was reinforce the mess I made of our friendship."

"No, it didn't. That questionnaire proved that our friendship was stronger than we gave it credit for. It also proved that I've had a pretty miserable year without you. I spent most of it telling myself otherwise, but, Jon, I don't want a world without you in it."

I wondered if he was ruminating on this or had dozed off. Just when I thought it was the latter, Jon said, "You need to do what's best for *you*, Sage. If all you want or can handle is a friendship, then I can accept that."

I fiercely envied him for his ability to surrender at that moment. Could almost feel the room tilt like a teeter-totter, his side lighter with all the weight on mine.

And then it hit me: here was my heart, an open target with a bull's-eye as big as the sky. It became clear that I had to keep it open, defenseless. If I was going to get past this fear, if I was going to truly let go and trust, I had to do the only thing left to do. Lean in. Exactly what Hazel had told me to do. It also became clear that there was no other way to love and be loved. You couldn't have earth-spinning love without that raw vulnerability. It was beyond fragile, yes. But for the first time in my life, I saw that it was also beautiful. Because that's what I had seen when I looked into Jonathan's eyes tonight.

If you offer someone your love for the right reasons and with the right intention, you can't lose.

At midnight, fireworks popped and boomed and sprinkled colors cascaded through the crack in the drapes.

I folded back the covers, sat up and swung my legs around to the edge of the bed, touched the industrial carpet with my bare feet, and, in two steps, scooted myself onto Jon's bed and pressed against him. He stirred and turned to face me. I could barely make out the contour of his face, which I cupped with my hand.

"Happy New Year, Jonathan," I said, and placed my lips on his.

CHAPTER TWENTY-THREE

Confession: Love scenes are always my favorite to write. They're the ultimate challenge in sensory description and using language to show rather than explain what the characters are feeling, from both a tactile and emotional sense. Plus, you want your reader reaching for something to fan herself with as opposed to, say, something else to read.

Some of the best love scenes I've ever written were actually quite chaste. There's something to be said for "less is more." But readers have criticized me for raising too many expectations. One woman stood up in a book club I was visiting—*stood up* with wineglass in hand—and laid into me: "Really, who has sex that good? You can't do that to us. Just once I'd like to see a sex scene in which the man just grunts and rolls over and is asleep in five minutes while you're just lying there, finishing the job. Again."

The woman's fellow book-clubbers cheered and applauded and raised their glasses to her.

"It's a *love* scene, not a *sex* scene," I'd said in response. "It's about *intimacy*. And the best part of novel writing—and reading—is going where you can't in reality. The sex can be as tantalizing or as humdrum as you want it to be. And, as you just highlighted, who wants humdrum sex? Or, more specifically, who wouldn't want great sex? Better yet, who doesn't want sex that is the result of a man looking into your eyes and knowing—just *knowing*—you're the reflection of everything that is right in his world? Who doesn't want her cheek caressed as he whispers 'I love you' and then levels you when he pulls you into his warmth and says, 'When you're in my arms, everything is right in my world'?"

The room had become pin-droppingly quiet. I don't know if I'd depressed the shit out of them or given them food for thought and they were still chewing.

Here's how my love scene with Jonathan Moss played out: his warm, dry lips covered mine, and when I parted them wider, he slid his tongue inside. We curled up into each other. Being in Jon's arms under the covers was like cuddling up with a space heater in a down sleeping bag. He kissed me again and moved his hand across my torso before cupping my breast through my shirt. I lifted my shirt and reapplied his hand to said breast.

"Do you really want to do this?" he asked while he dabbled my nipple with his finger.

"I wouldn't be here if I didn't, and you wouldn't be having such a good time right now," I teased.

"No, I mean, is it *OK*?"

I caressed the contour of his face with the back of my hand, his coarse beard scratching against it, and whispered, "It's OK," because it was. I knew it now. We weren't crossing a line, or going past the point of no return. We were neither too soon nor too late. We weren't becoming more than friends. We were already more.

We smiled.

Kisses. Beginning with the shoulder he'd ogled the previous night, then moving from neck to shoulder to shoulder to chest to hips to thigh to ankle to toes and back again. Damn, he was good.

I kissed him hard as I wrapped my leg around his, and then he pulled me on top of him. We slowly found a rhythm, and I watched his eyes contentedly trace the curves of my body, his fingers following suit, as we moved and breathed and worked up a sweat. We climaxed and exhaled several deep breaths of satisfaction before I gingerly climbed off and lay beside him, his full-sized body spooning mine, our skin warm and sticky.

We were quiet until he said, "The fireworks stopped."

In a perfectly timed beat, I quipped, "Both of 'em," which prompted giggles.

He nuzzled me. "You're my best friend."

Sleeping with your best friend didn't have to be the end of the road, I realized. It could be the beginning of an entirely new one. Better yet, it could be the same road, moving forward. Together.

I practically purred. "And you're mine."

I don't think I would have done the moment justice in a novel. Some things just can't be put into words.

CHAPTER TWENTY-FOUR

January 1: New Year's Day

The alarm on Jon's phone trilled at 6:00 a.m. We groaned and he tapped the "Snooze" button on the screen. Still naked, I snuggled up to him and moved my foot along his leg. He murmured and stirred, then smiled when he saw me, tangled hair and morning breath and all, and wrapped himself around me.

January 1, 2017.

New year. New day.

God, the metaphor thumped me like a mallet. What was New Year's Day if not an annual do-over? A chance to live a better, healthier, more fulfilling life. Leaving the previous year behind. Promise. Hope. Dread, even, for some.

We didn't linger in bed as we'd wanted to, however. Instead, we were determined to be on the road in time to make it to Sacramento and the memorial. We showered and dressed and ate breakfast in the hotel restaurant before loading Penelope and hitting the highway around eight thirty.

A playlist of Simple Minds, New Order, Prince, and Thompson Twins, compiled by yours truly, allowed us to bypass conversation for the first hour. Just as well—my stomach was already twisting in anticipation of showing up at the memorial and facing Kathleen. I had failed to consider what it would be like to listen to Kathleen, or whoever, spew out my father's achievements while omitting his failures. Knowing her, she'd leave out the part about his abandoning Mom and Gaia and me. Would leave Gaia and me out altogether.

I was about to attend the memorial of a man I didn't know at all. A man who had been my father in fact rather than deed.

Kathleen had no idea I was coming. I wanted to catch her off guard. For once, I wanted the upper hand. I'd been mentally composing things I wanted to say to her following the memorial: *How exactly did that work—you and my father erasing all traces of his family? Was it a systematic thing, or did it happen gradually? Was it planned from the get-go? Was it your idea or his? Or was it a united front? Did you ever stop to think about how a ten-year-old would be affected by her father's abandonment? Or her twelve-year-old sister? Did you ever consider the* cruelty *of it? Did you ever consider the cruelty of informing your husband's daughters of his death after he was cremated? Did you not care that you'd robbed them of the chance to pay their respects, even though he certainly never paid them an ounce of respect while he was alive?*

Holy shit. That was an ammunition round of anger.

And where would I go to say to my father, *Thanks to you, I spent my entire life afraid to truly love anyone. Thanks to you, I was afraid to love my best friend . . . ?*

"Penny for your thoughts," said Jon. I hadn't realized how far away I'd strayed in my own head.

I turned off the music. "I've been thinking about things," I started.

"Me too," he said.

"You first," I lobbed.

He placed his hand on my leg, and my hand fell over it.

"You and I have a lot in the bank," he said.

"Yes, we do."

"And aside from you needing to stand on tiptoes to hug or kiss me, we fit together well."

"You calling me short, Mossy?"

"Nah, I'm calling me a big galoot."

"Well, yeah."

He grinned and I squeezed his hand.

"Seriously, what are you trying to tell me?" I asked.

"The thing we fear most in a relationship is getting hurt. And we're afraid of getting hurt the next time, and the next. But I've come to see it like getting a rejection letter from an agent or an editor, or a bad review. It sucks. But that rejection isn't who we are. We keep writing. We keep telling stories. And what one person rejects, another accepts."

"Didn't I use that analogy in one of my novels?"

"You did. In *Deep Cuts*."

"You plagiarized me?" I said in mock outrage.

"I only steal the really good shit."

I met his self-effacing expression with a playful sneer.

I ruminated on this theory. Whenever I received a rejection in writing, I'd always managed to separate the writing from me. But rejection in love was way more personal. If I did the breaking up, I shrugged it off. But when someone dumped me, it signaled some major flaw in me. I dished out the advice in my debut novel, *Deep Cuts*, about a hairdresser-turned-author, but I forgot to apply it to me.

And for the first time, I saw Jonathan's letter in a new light. He wasn't rejecting me. I hadn't done anything wrong. In fact, I'd done everything *right*.

And if that was the case, then maybe the same was true with my father. I didn't do anything wrong. I was simply *me*, and he left anyway.

It didn't mean I was less than. It meant he made a stupid choice. I mean, really, how is a ten-year-old responsible for a grown-up behaving badly?

Jon was the only person who had seen the real me—even before we saw each other face-to-face. That's why it had devastated me when he sent that letter.

"Are you anticipating that we're going to hurt each other again?" I asked.

He shook his head. "The opposite. I think all our past hurts and rejections brought us to this point. You have to admit, this road trip gave us a glimpse of what life could be like for us."

"Everyday life won't be playlists and questionnaires."

"No, but it will be relationship building. It'll be like a game of HORSE. We each take our shots. Hit some and miss some. And the more we play, the better we get."

"You paint a nice picture, Mossy. But what about the big thing—where do we live?"

He frowned. "Let's wait till we get to Tacoma before we address that."

"OK," I said, already dreading it.

The car cruised for several miles.

"Do you think I'm making a mistake by showing up at this memorial?" I asked.

"I really don't know," he said. "Do you?"

"If I don't show up, I'll feel like I chickened out, and I'll hate myself for that. I'll feel like Kathleen somehow won and got the best of me again. But I'm afraid of what I'll find when I get there. A man—or the retrospect of the life of a man—who never gave me a second thought. I wanted answers as to why. But Gaia was right. I won't get them."

"You won't know either way unless you show up," Jon offered. "And even if Gaia is right, what's the worst that happens?"

"I get hurt all over again."

"And then what? You're still here. You're still this beautiful, intelligent, sexy, talented woman I'm in love with."

My heart was so raw and open, and his words covered it like aloe over a burn. The healing property wasn't in their coming from him, but rather in their truth.

Soothed, I closed my eyes and eventually fell into a deep sleep. Didn't open them again until noon.

We stopped for lunch around one thirty, making small talk as we ate. Now that we were done with the questionnaire, I wondered if we had finally run out of things to talk about. However, I noticed the fullness and warmth of our eye contact. The softened smiles and knowing glances. The simplicity of his hand in mine wherever we went, even if only a few feet from Penelope to the door of a convenience store.

After lunch, we sat in the SUV, and I waited for him to turn the key. He looked at me.

"Want to take over for a bit?"

"Driving? Penelope? For real?" I asked.

He nodded. "I need to close my eyes."

I went slack-jawed. "Wow, I had no idea sex would be so influential."

He smiled wearily.

I hopped out, jaunted to the other side, passing him along the way, and hopped back in, adjusting the seat and mirrors and resetting the GPS. Before I started the car, I said, "Honestly, do you really trust me?"

"I do," he said. "Even if I weren't so sleepy. I trust you to drive my car. I trust you with everything."

Damn if that didn't make me feel valuable.

I put Penelope in gear and tentatively stepped on the gas. Jon was asleep within minutes. We were still holding hands.

Chapter Twenty-Five

One closed highway, two wrong turns, and a confused GPS took us far enough off range that we didn't arrive at the Golf Club (and what an odd choice of venue for a memorial service) until 3:47 p.m. I didn't know how long memorial services typically lasted, but I was guessing we'd be walking in on the tail end.

Jon took in the surroundings. "This parking lot looks pretty deserted."

"Maybe we missed it," I said.

"I'm so sorry, Sage."

"It's not your fault," I said. "Shit happens."

And man, did it feel shitty.

We walked toward the doors. My stomach lurched with every step. Jon tentatively took hold of the handle, as if testing whether the door was locked, before pulling it open. We entered to utter silence, and Jon poked around while I lingered behind. Down the hallway, he found a sign with an arrow pointing left: "Merriweather Memorial Service."

Jon gripped my hand and practically pulled me toward the second entrance; my feet seemed stuck to the floor.

"Ready?" he whispered. I sucked in a breath and nodded. We entered the room.

Two men were folding chairs. A wreath of flowers hung behind an empty lectern.

Jon released my hand and approached one of the men. "Excuse me," he said softly. "Is the Merriweather service over?"

"Yeah, you missed it," said the man. His voice was gruff. "Let out fifteen minutes ago. No one showed up."

Jon didn't bat an eye. I, on the other hand, was stunned. "None at all?" he asked.

"Just the wife," said the man. "And a few others who came and went. I felt bad for her. That's got to suck, but who schedules a memorial service on New Year's Day?"

"Maybe it was the only day the venue was available?" posited Jon.

The other man shook his head. "I knew Tom. He didn't have many friends."

"Why was that?" asked Jon.

The man shrugged. "I don't think it was because of him as much as his wife. She's an odd one. Treated the whole thing like an afterthought. Don't know why she even bothered, other than to have it in the bulletin."

"Did she give any remarks?" said Jon. You'd think he was interviewing the men for a newspaper article.

The second man shrugged. "Don't know. I didn't stay either. Had to work. She turned on the waterworks every time someone entered the room, though. That I saw."

"You make it sound like she was disingenuous. Her husband died," said Jon.

"No," I finally chimed in. "That's Kathleen all the way."

"You had to be there," said the second man. "She was stone-faced one minute. And the next minute someone walked in, she wailed. I'm telling you, it wasn't grief. It was showmanship. You just know when someone's faking it."

I'd heard enough. "Let's go, Jon," I said. To the men, I said, "Thank you for your time."

"Did you know Tom?" asked the first man.

"No, I didn't," I said, and walked out.

"Thank you," said Jon, and he followed me out.

I plodded to the car and stepped in after Jon unlocked it. Once inside, I buried my face in my hands and cried. For what? I wondered. Because I missed the memorial? Because my father—*Tom*—had a lousy turnout? Because Kathleen didn't even care to stick around for a full hour?

Jon reached past me and pulled a wad of napkins out of the glove box. He took one and wiped the tears from my cheeks.

"I'm sorry, honey," he said. *Honey.* The affection behind the word was just as sweet as the real thing.

"I don't even know what I'm crying about," I said.

"It's a sad thing to know a person died alone."

"It's karma," I said. "I should get some satisfaction from that. But it feels positively shitty."

"You didn't abandon him, Sage. You showed up."

"I showed up too late. In every way, I was too late."

He nestled my cheek and chin in his hand. "What do you want to do now?"

I sniffled and dried my eyes. "I want to go to his house."

"Why?"

"To prove that he lived there. That he had a life."

I told Jon the address, and he entered it into the GPS. Ten minutes later, we pulled up to the curb of the mid-twentieth-century ranch house. I didn't see any cars in the driveway, but that didn't mean Kathleen wasn't home.

He killed the ignition, and we sat in stillness so deafening you'd think time had stopped. The butterflies I'd had in the Phoenix airport were nothing compared to the pterodactyls presently circling in my gut.

I'd never been to this house before. The painted gray façade and white door were faded, even peeling on the shutters. Rosebushes wilted, either dormant or dead—hard to tell. The lawn was small, lackluster, an empty bird feeder sitting front and center. I tried to imagine what kind of living had taken place inside for the last twenty years. What would I find? Would it be as unkempt as the outside? Or would it be the opposite? Would the shelves be crammed with books, like in my house? Would the kitchen table be cluttered with mail and newspapers and coffee cups? Would photos or artwork adorn the walls? What kind of taste did my father have in art? Or books? Or cooking?

I just sat and stared and churned.

"You sure you want to do this?" Jon asked.

"No," I said.

He rested his arm around my shoulders after stroking my hair.

"What if she's not home?" he asked.

"I don't know."

"No rule that says you have to do this. No one will be the wiser."

"Except me. And Gaia. I couldn't not tell her. And you."

"Do you think I'd judge you for it?"

"No. But the whole point of my coming here was to do what I should have done while my father was still alive."

"But did you really *need* to do it? Was whatever you think you failed to do really *your* failure?"

No.

I looked at him, and he again brought his hand to my cheek in a caress. I mirrored the gesture.

"Sage, no matter what you decide to do, you're going to be OK. And I'm here for you. *I'm here.*"

"Thank you," I said, my voice choking.

I opened the car door. Jon followed. We met at the bottom of the cement driveway full of cracks, joined hands, and headed up the walk. When we reached the door, I took another deep breath, knocked five times, and waited, squeezing Jonathan's hand as if it were a stress ball.

No answer.

I knocked again.

Nothing.

I pressed the doorbell and a tired, muffled chime responded.

Just as I turned around and said, "Let's go," to Jon, the door whisked open. Startled, I faced a white-haired, wrinkled and pale, bespectacled Kathleen in a knitted olive-green cardigan. For a split second I thought she had donned a wig and makeup until I realized time had caught up to her since I'd last seen her, when I was in my early twenties.

"Hi, Kathleen," I said. I couldn't feign friendliness even if I'd tried.

She squinted through her bifocals at me, then Jon, and back to me.

"Sage Merriweather. Tom's daughter."

The same age trick having just been presumably played on her as well, she finally registered recognition. "Oh. Sage. What are you doing here?"

I became a statue, and the world around me stood still again.

What was I doing here?

My father was dead. He'd been dead a lot longer than six weeks.

During that time I'd grown up, graduated from both college and cosmetology school, wrote four novels—one of them a bestseller, made friends all over the country, and in the last three days alone, saw the Grand Canyon, the Pacific Ocean, three states, and fell in love.

I'd been rejected, and I was OK.

I'd lost jobs, and I was OK.

I'd had book proposals and queries turned down, and I was OK.

I'd had one-star reviews, and I was OK.

I had a mother and a sister who would walk through fire for me. Who *did* walk through fire *with* me.

I had a best friend who took a second chance on once in a lifetime.

All my life I'd thought my happiness was dependent on my father's love and acceptance and presence. But my stories told otherwise. Real and fiction, they depicted characters of strength. Characters of tenacity. Characters with a voice. I'd spent a lifetime controlling the outcome of said stories because I couldn't control the outcome of what I'd believed to be the most important one.

And now, standing on that stoop with a faded welcome mat and a barren planter with dried soil, it became clear that whereas I had spent my life attending to my clients and my characters and my readers and my friends and my family and my hair and my books and my world, my father and Kathleen had lived a life of neglect and abandonment and carelessness. What's more, I finally realized that my happiness was *never* dependent on him. Or Jonathan Moss. Or Gaia or Mom or anyone else but *me*.

At that moment, I let go of Jon's hand and looked Kathleen squarely in the eye.

"I have no idea," I said.

And with that I pivoted, ambling back down the path and the driveway to Penelope, my lover by my side. Kathleen closed the door.

Jon unlocked the car door and I stepped in, exhaling as I pulled the seat belt across my chest. When he slid in, he looked at me tentatively.

"You OK?" he asked.

"You know, it's funny. She closed the door just now. I didn't. *She* did. But I'm the one who walked away first. Because I can't close something that was never open," I said.

Jon nodded and took my hand in his, but I gently released it. "Thank you," I said. "But I don't need consolation. Please understand, I'm appreciative. I really am. You've been such a loving support today.

Not to mention a great friend. But this is no longer on you. It's no longer on me either. It's hers now."

"OK," he said. "I'm proud of you. I would have been no matter how this went."

I smiled. "Let's get back on the road." Then I lowered the window to let in the sun and breeze as Jon pulled away from the house, and Sacramento, for good.

CHAPTER TWENTY-SIX

January 2

The scenery along the way to Eugene, Oregon, was spellbinding, with big skies and flat plains, but desolate, save for grazing cows. Jon and I took turns driving again, listened to music and sang out loud to prevent sleepiness, and stopped for bathroom breaks and gas fill-ups and to stretch our legs. When we finally reached our destination, we found a Best Western and checked in and lugged our stuff to the room and used the bathroom and brushed our teeth and peeled off our clothes and went to bed—a king-size—and fell asleep with Jon spooning me, one arm under the pillow cradling my head and the other across my chest, his body cocooning mine. It didn't feel like cloud nine, or that kind of in-love feeling when your heart is going to fall out of your chest from the magnitude of it all, or when you feel as if you can soar through space. No, this felt grounding, down to earth, like we'd slept this way, together, all our lives.

Dare I say, like home.

We reached Portland the following afternoon. Ate lunch al fresco at the food truck park despite the temperatures turning chilly, followed by a romp through the legendary Powell's bookstore, an amusement park for bibliophiles. We spotted our titles and snapped boastful self-ies with them, then disappeared in the stacks and managed to meet at the cash wrap at the same time, unplanned, with armloads of books. It also turned out that among the trove, we each bought a book for the other. For Jon, I selected a used collection of Encyclopedia Brown stories—he'd pored through them (and solved the "mysteries") by the time he was eight years old. For me, Jon chose an early printing of Judy Blume's *It's Not the End of the World*, remembering the story I had told him about having read it repeatedly until the spine had finally given out when I was eleven years old. Inside he inscribed:

To Sage: Thank you for the journey. Love, Jon

My eyes welled up when I read it.

"I didn't even think to inscribe yours," I said, feeling foolish.

"You didn't have to," he said. "Your thoughtfulness was enough. And I was afraid choosing this particular book would bring back bad memories for you."

"Reading that book incessantly was the way I grieved my parents' divorce," I said. "Or at least, one part of it. The other was that I wrote my own stories. Secret stories that to this day, no one has ever seen. Even I haven't read them since. God, they're like, thirty-five years old now."

"What were they about?"

"Some were about a child who gets her parents back together. I remember another was about a girl who finds a bag of money and becomes president—funny the things an eleven-year-old comes up with."

"Not too far from how elections work today," he said.

"Those were the first stories I wrote where I realized writing equaled power. If my real life was shitty, then I'd make up one that was downright magical. If my father left, then I'd write a story where a father returns and promises never to leave again. In my teens, the daughter got revenge by being rich and famous and getting the rock-star boyfriend. Bad writing, of course. But Freud would have been salivating over it."

Jon cupped my face with his hands, leaned down, and kissed me. "You're wonderful," he said.

I beamed. "So are you."

"Of course by *wonderful*, I mean *fucked up*," he added after a beat.

"Well, yeah," I replied. "So are you."

We exited Powell's with tote bags of books slung over our shoulders and giddy smiles plastered on our faces.

We reached Tacoma as the sun set, casting a pink glow over Mount Rainier against a blue-purple sky with striped clouds so perfect I thought the image was a hologram or a painted mural. On the other side, Commencement Bay, as vast and blue as Long Island Sound. Tacoma was, as Jon explained it, Seattle's little brother, always getting teased and passed over for being too scrawny. Precisely why Jon felt drawn to it, I'm sure. Well, that, and the mountain—er, volcano.

He drove us through downtown and pulled into a restaurant on the water called the Lobster Shop. Cornball name, I thought, until we stepped inside. I felt self-consciously underdressed in a hoodie, jeans, and Uggs, sans makeup. Jon wore a fleece pullover and blue jeans yet still seemed to fit in despite most patrons decked out in dresses and Dockers and sport jackets. I pulled a tube of lipstick from my purse and applied it flawlessly under five seconds without a mirror. Little trick I perfected during my salon days.

"I know you're tired and wanted something more casual," he said. "But the food is so good, we needed to eat here before you fly back to New York tomorrow."

Tomorrow. Already. Funny how I hadn't thought once about returning to New York. Never counted down the days, hours, minutes. Never hoped it would come sooner. Now, however, it loomed like a clock ticking down to doomsday.

We were seated at a table overlooking the bay, now silhouetted in twilight. We savored and salivated over lobster bisque, grilled salmon with risotto, perfectly paired wine, and a flourless chocolate torte so decadent we practically orgasmed over every bite.

Jon looked at me, and the contented grin was back. "We made it, Sage. Not just through this road trip, but through the fuck-up-ery of this past year. I did a little happy dance in the stacks when we were at Powell's. Seriously, I did."

A tear slid down my cheek and dripped onto the empty dessert plate. All the burdens I'd carried—Jon's betrayal; my heartbreak, resistance, and confusion—instantly floated out of me, like steam rising off wet pavement following a rainstorm. We sat there, face-to-face, fixed and focused, and said so much without a single word.

After dinner, Jon drove us to his condo; he had pointed out the building to me on the way to the restaurant. As we unloaded Penelope and rode the elevator up, bone-tired, the dormant butterflies woke up. And apparently drank some coffee. The elevator stopped on the fifth floor and we stepped off as Jon jingled his keys until the right one presented itself. He unlocked the door and flipped on a light.

He had bought the condo upon first moving to Tacoma—a two-bedroom, one-bathroom spread, complete with washer-dryer hookup and an open-concept living/dining area and fully applianced kitchen—brand-new, sight unseen, for a price that would make New Yorkers slobber with envy. In terms of square footage, the space fell short in comparison to the house I rented in Port Jefferson, but the view! Mount

Rainier on one side of the building and the bay on the other. His was the Rainier side. It was the side he wanted, the side he paid for. I would have opted for the opposite, I remarked.

I couldn't help but inspect the rooms with a purpose. We were officially on Jon's turf now, a potentially life-changing conversation looming, and whether I could envision myself living there might give me insight to the direction that conversation would take. The furniture was scant, pieces scraped together. Overflowing bookcases and basic table lamps from Target. A secondhand coffee table. Impressive sectional and wall-mounted TV set. Bare cream walls save a couple pieces of artwork from vendors in Seattle's Pike Place Market. Snapshots of his nieces and nephews taped to his refrigerator door. Jon led me to the bedroom with my stuff and flipped on yet another light, revealing a king-size bed sparsely adorned with a beloved gray comforter and two pillows, flanked by only one end table, and a smaller TV sitting atop a cheap put-it-together chest of drawers.

Could definitely use a woman's touch—rather, *my* touch. Pops of color in things you normally wouldn't pay attention to: light and outlet wall plates, lampshades, and pillowcases. More photographs and artwork. Floor-length drapes. Warm tones, like a southwestern sunset, for example, for the walls.

"As you can see, it's all very postdivorce," said Jon apologetically.

"It feels transient to me," I said, crossing my arms as if warding off a chill. "I don't mean that as a criticism. Just an observation."

He nodded. "I miss my dog. Still expect him to greet me at the door."

"I'm sorry," I said. After a beat, I asked, "Will you get another?"

"Eventually."

"And will you stay here?"

I said *you*, but I was thinking *we*. *Would we stay here? Would I be able to?*

"I do love this place. I missed the extra income when I was subletting it, but I have no plans to move."

"Why didn't you and Shannon live here?"

"We did before we were married. But Shannon hated the location. She wanted something more suburban. A house, proverbial picket fence, yada yada yada."

I found myself secretly agreeing with Shannon. Something about a detached house with a yard and basement and attic . . . maybe it was all the apartment living I'd done. Or maybe it was how I pictured married life, or rather, the picture I'd known before my father left.

Late at night, in bed, after watching several episodes of *The Mary Tyler Moore Show* from Jon's DVD collection, he clicked off the TV and we lay curled together, naked, in the dark. He peppered my neck and shoulders with kisses.

"I wish you didn't have to leave," he said in a near whisper.

"Me neither," I replied. The harshness of the word *leave*—the finality it carried—left me grasping for another way to cast it. Or toss it altogether.

"You could change your flight."

"I could," I started, "but . . ." I didn't know how to finish. These incredible days were over and we had to either go back to Facebook and texting or start something completely new. But how? How did that work? How did I start over without giving up everything and everyone I knew and loved? What if he didn't want to either?

Jon interrupted the feelings I was trying to put into words. "Can you see yourself living here?"

I waited for what felt like a long time to reply. "No."

He exhaled a deflated breath. "Why not?"

"It's not home," I said. The words sucked the life force out of me.

"You haven't given it a chance. Don't you think it could be?"

"Can you see yourself living on Long Island?" I asked.

He took just as long as I did to respond. "No," he said. Before I could ask why not, he said, "Same reason."

"Should we flip a coin?" I asked, half-sarcastic.

"Doesn't seem to be any other way."

"It won't solve the problem of one of us living somewhere he or she doesn't want to be," I said. "That can't make for a solid relationship. One person can't make all the sacrifice."

"Maybe we can find a way to have both," he said. "Live in both places. Three months on Long Island, three months in Tacoma, and then switch off again."

"Do you know how expensive it would be to fly back and forth and maintain two homes, at least one of them empty for three months at a time? How do we determine seasons? How do we decide on holidays? We'll go broke in a year."

"I'm trying to find a solution," he said. "There's got to be one that works for both of us."

I racked my brain until a dull headache emerged.

"I don't think there is one," I said.

He looked utterly defeated. "So what do we do?" he asked.

I sighed. "Hold each other until we fall asleep."

CHAPTER TWENTY-SEVEN

Whereas I'd spent most of the flight to Phoenix in anticipation of what and whom I would be meeting, I spent the flight back to New York distraught over what and whom I left behind. I leaned my head against the covered window, exhausted, isolated, and lonely as hell, as I replayed Jon's and my good-bye at SeaTac: escorting me to the ticket counter, assisting me with my luggage, and then the two of us standing at the security gate, our hands needing to be pulled apart.

"This totally sucks, Moss," I said in an attempt to downplay the moment of our having to say the actual word: *good-bye.*

He wasn't buying it. Took my face into his chaliced hands and kissed me repeatedly. "Please don't go," he begged, bringing his forehead to mine. "I'll reimburse your ticket. Renegotiate your deadline. Fly your mom and sister here. Anything."

"We'll figure something out," I said. "Promise. In the meantime, I'll meet you at LaGuardia in a month."

His longing, watchful eye followed me until I was past security, on my way to the gate. He blew a kiss in response to my wave seconds before I was out of his sight.

Leaving Jonathan Moss behind was like being on a ship sinking into the dark-blue depths.

He texted me within minutes: `I hate this.`

~

For days upon returning, I meandered about my empty house, completing tasks somewhat robotically—unpacking and catching up on laundry, cleaning, grocery shopping—and staring out the window more than at my computer screen, looking for a big sky, failing to conjure the sight of a mountain. I went to Sag Harbor and walked up and down Main Street, shielding myself from the biting wind on the wharf. The tree lights were gone. The menorah in front of the old windmill removed. The wreaths on storefront doors dried up. Olaf's ice-cream shop had been closed since Labor Day weekend. I found myself craving lobster bisque and risotto.

I missed Jon's face and the sound of his voice. I missed the taste of his mouth and the smell of his skin. I missed the warmth of his arms. I missed our legs brushing against each other whenever we sat side by side. I missed the simple moments—a pat on the arm, a knowing glance, saying the same thing at the same time. I missed the hum of Penelope. I missed his breath on the back of my neck.

We'd texted and FaceTimed since my return to New York, but it was so two-dimensional and insufficient now. Not to mention I'd slept horridly since leaving his bed.

"So how was your trip?" my mom asked one week later. We sat in the Golden Pear café sipping lattes and splitting a blueberry muffin.

"It was good," I said. "I saw some cool stuff. The Grand Canyon, the Pacific Ocean, Powell's bookstore."

"How did things go with your friend?"

"Well, we patched things up," I started.

"That's good," she said. "Although I can't help but feel like there's more."

Moms. Can't put anything past them.

I looked directly at her. "I want to be with Jon," I said. "I'm in love with him. He's in love with me. But we just can't."

"Why?"

I waved my arm in a panorama. "Here," I said. "This is stopping me. He wants to live in Tacoma, and I want to live here."

"Sage, don't throw tomorrow away because you're stuck in yesterday. It's OK to let go. I'll be fine. Gaia will be fine. The island isn't going anywhere."

"Gee, thanks," I said. "Glad I'm so expendable."

Mom took my hand. "You know I'm not saying that. You've lived away from home before."

"In college," I said. "You think I came back because the cost of living was so great? I *love* it here, Mom."

She folded her hands on the table. "Well, then that's that. I guess you can find a nice man here in town instead."

For a fleeting moment, I considered it. Imagined someone other than Jon and me smelling books as we browsed in the bookstore or the library. Or on dates at the Golden Pear. A play at the Bay Street Theater. Perhaps. But I never wanted to shoot hoops with anyone else. I never wanted to take a trip with anyone else. I never wanted to look at Steinbeck's house with anyone else. I never wanted to share bad pizza or watch *South Park* or see the Grand Canyon or spend hours on end in a car with anyone else.

I never asked anyone else who he'd want to have dinner with, living or dead. I never asked anyone else his best and worst memory. I never asked anyone else what his idea of a perfect day looked like.

Mom asked one last question. "What makes him the sure thing?"

At that moment, a rush of calm overcame me. "Because we could let each other go and be OK."

And then it happened. The master key. Jonathan Moss wasn't the reason I'd been miserable a year ago, and he wasn't the reason for my happiness now. Nor was he responsible for it. What a weight to dump on any one person. Taking the road trip, putting my past to rest, making things right with Jon—I did it for *me*, just as he'd gone to therapy and repaired his life for *him*. And because I did, I fell in love. With my best friend. Sure, I could stay here and he could stay there, and we'd be fine.

But I didn't want that.

I finally owned it. And it was the best feeling in the world.

Chapter Twenty-Eight

The morning after breakfast with my mother, I called Jon. Eleven o'clock my time; eight o'clock his. I sat on my bed in Port Jefferson, propped against the pillows, wearing the sweatshirt he'd given me at the Grand Canyon. Still smelled like him.

"I was about to call you," he said after the second ring.

"I have to tell you something."

I pictured him bracing himself.

"I've been all over the island this past week," I started. "Drove around my old neighborhood. Went to my favorite places. Walked miles of beach. Wandered aimlessly from room to room of my house. Even took the train to and from Manhattan. And here's the thing: it's not home anymore. Not without you. Home was that Comfort Inn in Eugene. It was Original Joe's in San Jose. The basketball court in Las Vegas. Pismo Beach in the dead of December. Your parents' house in Phoenix. Home is wherever you are, Jon. It's wherever *we* are."

He paused to catch his breath.

"I was about to tell you the exact same thing," he said.

I gasped and covered my mouth with my hand before placing it over my rapidly beating heart.

"Figures you'd try to one-up me, Moss."

I could hear his smile, could feel the warmth radiating from him. "At least I didn't wager anything this time."

Chapter Twenty-Nine

A week later, somewhere over Lake Michigan, we sat side by side, our legs brushing up against each other, seat belts buckled. Fingers laced together as we looked out the window, a carpet of cloud covering a morning sky drenched in pastels of orange and pink and blue. No Xanax knockoff this time. I wasn't afraid.

He nudged his head against mine and kissed my nose. "I love you, Sage."

"I love you, Jon."

Five miles high, yet completely grounded. On our way home.

ACKNOWLEDGMENTS

The year 2016 so far has been a whirlwind. Mostly magical and magnificent yet also stressful to the hilt at times. As a writer, I gained a wealth of new memories and experiences to draw on for future stories. But in terms of focus, my craft and process were challenged in ways I hadn't anticipated.

I am grateful to the following people for taking the journey with me:

Miriam Juskowicz, my acquisitions editor, for accepting me into her care and patiently working with me to make sure this book would be delivered on time and in its best incarnation.

Tiffany Yates Martin, the personal trainer of developmental editors, who not only pushed me hard but also held my hand. This book wouldn't have stood a chance without her. Bonus points for some of the funniest editorial comments ever to be written in all caps.

Nalini Akolekar, my literary agent, for believing in me and guiding me through new territory.

Jessica Poore, who played matchmaker for Nalini and me. Fitting, considering it happened during the Romance Writers of America conference in New York City.

Gabriella Dumpit and the entire staff at Lake Union Publishing, who make me proud and happy to be a part of their team.

The Undeletables, just because. Ditto for Ru.

My dear friends in Billings, Montana, who welcomed me into their loving fold from the moment I arrived.

My mom, Reverend Eda Lorello, for putting up with my profanity during those long car trips, and my siblings, nieces, and nephews, for loving me always.

My parents-in-law: Leslie and Charles Clines, and Ron Lancaster; and my siblings-, nieces-, and nephews-in-law. I couldn't have joined a better clan.

My readers, for being so incredibly patient.

And Craig, my dearest love: "You'll never see the end of the road while you're traveling with me."

If I've left anyone out (and I almost always do, dammit), then please know you're in my heart, and my gratitude abounds.

About the Author

Elisa Lorello is a Long Island native, the youngest of seven children. She earned her bachelor's and master's degrees at the University of Massachusetts Dartmouth and taught rhetoric and writing at the college level for more than ten years. In 2012 she became a full-time novelist.

Elisa is the author of seven novels, including the bestselling *Faking It*, and one memoir. She has been featured in the *Charlotte Observer* and the Raleigh *News & Observer* and was a guest speaker at the Triangle Association of Freelancers 2012 and 2014 Write Now! conferences. In May 2016 she presented a lesson for the Women's Fiction Writers Association spring workshop. She continues to speak and write about her publishing experience and also teaches the craft of writing and revision.

Elisa enjoys reading, walking, hanging out in coffee shops, Nutella, and all things Duran Duran. She plays guitar badly and occasionally draws. She moved to Montana in 2016 and is newly married.

Connect with Elisa:
On Facebook at Elisa Lorello, Author
On Twitter @elisalorello
Visit her website: elisalorello.com